Agnes
the Sheep

Also by William Taylor:

Paradise Lane

Agnes the Sheep

William Taylor

AN
APPLE
PAPERBACK

SCHOLASTIC INC.
New York Toronto London Auckland Sydney

No part of this publication may be reproduced in whole or in part, or stored in a retrieval system, or transmitted in any form or by any means, electronic, mechanical, photocopying, recording, or otherwise, without written permission of the publisher. For information regarding permission, write to Ashton Scholastic Ltd., 165 Marna Road Panmure Auckland, Private Bag 1 Penrose Auckland 6, New Zealand.

ISBN 0-590-43364-4

Copyright © 1990 by William Taylor. All rights reserved. Published by Scholastic Inc., 555 Broadway, New York, NY 10012, by arrangement with Ashton Scholastic Ltd. APPLE PAPERBACKS is a registered trademark of Scholastic Inc.

12 11 10 9 8 7 6 5 4 3 2 1   5   4 5 6 7 8 9/9

Printed in the U.S.A.   40

Agnes
the Sheep

1
Old Mrs. Carpenter

Old Mrs. Carpenter was eighty-nine years of age when she died. She left behind for her nearest and not-too-dearest relatives her large house on Gladstone Road, everything inside the house and the land the house stood on. Mrs. Carpenter died peacefully in her sleep at the end of a full life and with few regrets about leaving this world.

Mrs. Carpenter also left behind Agnes, her pet sheep. "I want you to promise me something," she had said to Belinda and Joe not too long before she died. "I'll be going soon."

"Where to?" asked Belinda.

"Heaven," said Mrs. Carpenter firmly. "I am charging you two with looking after Agnes for the rest of her natural life."

"Hey! That doesn't seem too fair to me," said Joe.

"Why not, pray?" said Mrs. Carpenter. "You've had your money's worth out of me since first we

1

met. If I remember rightly, it was you who wanted something from me back then. If poor, dear Agnes suffers the misfortune of falling into the hands of my great-nephew, Derek, I would doubt that her life would be extended one little bit."

"But why charge us to do it?" asked Joe. "I don't mind looking after the old sheep but I don't think it's very fair we've got to pay you to do it."

Old Mrs. Carpenter looked at him over the top of her rimless glasses. "Keep your mouth shut, boy! That way you sound more intelligent."

Belinda looked at Joe. "All Mrs. Carpenter means is that she's making us responsible. We'll be responsible for looking after Agnes."

"That's right girl," said Mrs. Carpenter. "However, I haven't kicked the bucket yet."

"And you're not going to, Mrs. Carpenter. Not for a long time," said Belinda.

"We've all gotta go sometime," said Joe softly, "and she sure is old." He risked a sideways glance at Mrs. Carpenter.

"Old she may be but she's not deaf," said Mrs. Carpenter sharply. "I've had a few good innings and I don't suppose I can postpone the inevitable all that much longer."

"I just bet you're still around to get your telegram from the Queen. She sends everyone a telegram if they get to be a hundred," said Belinda.

"Very nice too," said Mrs. Carpenter, "but is it worth hanging round another eleven years, I ask myself? Now, call in Agnes. It's time for her bread and milk. If it weren't for that dear and faithful animal, I would have lost all faith in the goodness of human nature years ago."

By the time she died, Joe and Belinda had known Mrs. Carpenter for quite a while, a relationship that had come about almost by chance.

"I want you to finish off your study of our community by taking a close look at the needs of the elderly — the old folk of our town," Mrs. Robinson, their teacher, had said. "Find out what they think of life today. What was life like for them, the dear old souls, back in our wonderful pioneer days? Ah yes, class. There's much we can learn from them all."

"She sure should know," Joe had said somewhat unwisely. "I reckon she's one of them oldies."

"I think that's a horrible thing for Joe Walsh to say about you, Mrs. Robinson," Belinda had said, "and it's not even right! Well, it's not quite right. Not just yet, anyway."

"What do we mean by that, Belinda?" Mrs. Robinson asked rather cunningly. "That old age is not quite nice? Is that it?" She shook her head. "Oh, never mind. The way I feel most days — dragging myself out of bed in the mornings . . ." She shook her head again and then brightened up a bit. "I'll tell you what I'm going to do, class. I'm going to put you all in pairs. Belinda, my dear, I think it would be a nice idea for you and Joe to work together. I'm sure you'll both enjoy that!"

Mrs. Robinson beamed very broadly.

"Aw, gee," said Joe, "that's not fair."

"No, it's not," agreed Belinda.

"Yes it is," said Mrs. Robinson, and her beam became a wide grin. "Yes. I want all of you in pairs and I think I just might let you — apart from Joe and Belinda of course — choose with whom to work . . ."

"Choose with whom to work," said Joe, mimicking Mrs. Robinson who ignored him.

"I want all of you to get to know one of our elderly citizens. There's just so much we can learn from them," she repeated. "Find out their thoughts and feelings about life today. Most important, class, find out the changes they have seen in our town. What was life really like for them in those far-off, rugged, pioneer days with no washing machines and no television, jet planes or videos? So, what questions can we ask them? You tell me, class, and I'll write them up on the blackboard. We'll make up a sort of senior citizens' questionnaire. Now, before you all start to bombard me with what I know will be oodles of questions, I'm going to ask you to work out in your own minds how you might offer to help the elderly person you interview." Mrs. Robinson's enthusiasm grew. "It's important we all give back a little something in return for what we are asking. Now, class, bombard me with those questions," she finished.

For the first time in half an hour there was dead

silence in Room Five of St. Joseph's Convent School.

"You might as well know right now this very minute that I'm not going to work with you and I'm going to get my mum to write a note and say so," said Belinda to Joe. "She will, too. Besides, one look at you, Joe Walsh, would give any old person a fatal heart disease like smoking does and I'm not going to hang around and get the blame."

"Yeah," said Joe, "one look at you and they'd reckon they got a deadly disease already. Anyway, we could interview your mum. She's sure elderly and old."

"She is not elderly," said Belinda.

"If she's not elderly and old, then being your mum has made her look like that. She looks old enough to be my mum's mum. Or even older still. She could be my mum's mum's mum!" said Joe. "Everyone I know reckons you must be the oldest-looking family in the whole of our town. In the whole of our country. Even in the whole of our universe!"

"Mrs. Robinson!" Belinda called out. "Joe Walsh is saying very horrible and very brutal and very nasty things about my family and they're not true. You should just hear what he's saying and it's not right and I done nothing."

"I can see that, Belinda," said Mrs. Robinson cheerfully. "Now get on with it."

"I'm going to get my mum to write you a note, Mrs. Robinson," said Belinda.

"One more note won't hurt, Belinda. I've got just about enough letters from your mother to paper the walls of this classroom with already."

"You mean with which to paper the walls of this classroom. That's what you mean, Mrs. Robinson," said Joe. "I'm not going to do anything, anyway. I'm sure not going to do anything with her," he added.

"Neither am I," said Belinda.

"What's new?" asked Mrs. Robinson. "We're two terms into this year already and if I've had two weeks' work out of either of you in all that time I'd be surprised. I've had more effort from your mother, Belinda, with all her notes." Mrs. Robinson shook her head. "Why have I put you two together? I'll tell us all why. It's simply so the two of you won't get to spoil two other pairs. That's why!"

Joe looked at Belinda.

Belinda looked at Joe.

Joe drew a tic-tac-toe grid on the desk top and placed the first zero. Belinda put a cross. They played in silence, slowly. The game ended in a draw.

"Let's prove old Robinson wrong," said Belinda.

"Why?" asked Joe, surprised.

"Dunno really," said Belinda. "Let's just prove her wrong."

"Okay," said Joe. "C'mon."

"We can't," said Belinda. "It's still schooltime. We can't just go."

"Of course we can," said Joe. "We're going to find our old person. It's schoolwork. Why should we have to use our own time? C'mon."

"We're gonna find our oldie, Mrs. Robinson," he called out to their teacher. "Me and Belinda. Okay? We want to get out and get one before everyone else gets theirs first."

Mrs. Robinson breathed a sigh of great and contented relief as Joe and Belinda left the room.

Belinda and Joe found old Mrs. Carpenter. Not that she was too hard to find. Her house stood on its large, overgrown section just beyond the town's main shopping center. It occupied a site that the owners of the Food Giant Supermarket next door were quite anxious to acquire for car parking. Surrounded by trees and a high fence to keep out prying eyes, the property was entered by way of a pair of elegant, wrought-iron gates on which hung two small signs. One said simply, "Carpenter," and the other one, "Beware of the Dog. Enter at Own Risk."

"I'm not going in there," said Joe. "I know this guy and he once told me this was a witch's house and it's all haunted."

"You believed him?" Belinda looked at Joe. "Yeah. You would."

"Besides, there's a dog. That's what it says on that sign," said Joe, nodding towards it. "I don't like animals."

"I don't know why, 'coz you are one," said Belinda, "and there is not so a dog. That sign's just to keep out people like you who nick things."

"I'm not going in," Joe said again. "I read this story once. It was called 'Hansel and Gretel.' Real scary." Joe shuddered.

"Look," Belinda said patiently, "it was you who said we should give this dumb idea a go. This here is your first prize old lady in the whole town. She's sort of the boss of this town. Once she was, anyway. She's just about older than anyone else and I think she's even older than the town and I met her once."

"You did not," said Joe.

Belinda unlatched the gate and led the way in and up the dark of the drive towards the house that stood directly ahead. Somehow the traffic noise of the busy street outside was absorbed by the wild growth of the loamy garden.

Suddenly, "Baaa! Baaaa! Baaaaaa!" and a shape as overgrown as anything in that garden erupted, rocketlike and woolly, from beneath a cluster of hydrangea bushes coming into early leaf. Belinda stood rigid. Joe turned to run. His startled movement caught the attention of the woollen shape. Head lowered, the shaggy creature charged at him and caught him in full flight. Joe flew quite high and landed, more bewildered than hurt, in the middle of a group of three evergreen azaleas.

"Heel, I say! Heel, boy! Heeeeel!" they heard from above them. Then, "Come on up here. Come on, now. The two of you. Let me see what you look like before I phone through to the police. How dare you trespass on my private property! Answer me that! Can you read? Can you? No, of course you can't. This modern nonsense they call education wouldn't allow for anything as straightforward as that. Come here, I say!"

Belinda and Joe crept to the steps of the house. Standing on the verandah looking down on them was a tall, straight, black-clad and very old woman. She carried a walking stick and used it to conduct the interview rather than to assist her in moving about. Behind her, and now at heel, sat the largest, dirtiest and woolliest sheep either Belinda or Joe had ever seen. The sheep looked even angrier than the old woman.

"It's . . . it's not my fault," stammered Joe. "It was all her idea." He pointed to Belinda.

"It's . . . it's . . . not a dog," said Belinda, looking at the animal.

"Of course it's not a dog, girl," said the woman. "It's a sheep. Can't you tell the difference?"

"She means — it's because it says beware of your dog down by your gate. That's what it says. We seen it," said Joe.

"Is there any law that says I can't write exactly what I choose on my own gate? Is there? No, don't tell me. There probably is," said the old lady. "It's

9

time I wrote to the council again. They don't like my letters."

"Are you old Mrs. Carpenter?" asked Joe.

"My name is Carpenter," said the woman, "and apart from that it is up to me to label myself in whatever way I see fit." She scowled down at them. "What do you want?"

"Let's go," said Joe.

"Stay!" ordered Mrs. Carpenter.

"You can't stop us," said Joe.

"You're right," said Mrs. Carpenter. "I can't, but she can." She prodded the sheep with her stick. "Now tell me what you want before I get this good animal to give you the bum's rush off my property." She gave a half-chuckle, half-cackle. Joe was reminded of the fate of Hansel and Gretel.

Belinda took a deep breath and in a jumble of words explained the reason for their visit.

"Come inside!" ordered Mrs. Carpenter. "I'm not in the habit of conducting personal conversations on my doorstep."

Belinda and Joe edged a wary path around the sheep, which sat watching their every movement. "Down, boy!" ordered Mrs. Carpenter as the animal lumbered to its feet, its eyes on Joe.

"What's his name?" asked Belinda as they moved indoors. The sheep, now on its feet, followed them.

"It's not a him. It's a her," said Mrs. Carpenter. "Can't you tell the difference?"

"Not with all that wool," said Joe. "Besides, you

call him a boy. Why d'you do that?"

"I don't know," said Mrs. Carpenter. "Her name is Agnes."

"Agnes?" said Belinda. "What a funny name for a sheep. Never heard of no sheep called Agnes before."

"Unable to read and now showing a distinct lack of general knowledge." Mrs. Carpenter shook her head. "What are we paying teachers for?"

"That's what I often think," said Joe. "You're quite right, Mrs. Carpenter. What are we paying them for?"

"Shut up, boy!" said Mrs. Carpenter. "Sit, Agnes!" and the sheep sat. "Lamb of God," she announced. "Lamb of God."

"Eh?" said Joe.

"That's what it means. Agnes. Lamb of God." She prodded at the heap of wool.

"That's really lovely," said Belinda. "Lamb of God. I think I might have heard that somewhere before. Just a dear old pet sheep what's a gift from our Father in Heaven."

"She was," said Mrs. Carpenter sharply. "This sheep was a gift from Allied Farmers' Transport whose drivers have always used this street as a racetrack. Clearly, one of them loaded one too many of the poor beasts on the top deck of his truck, took that wicked corner too wide and too fast and Agnes, bless her, flew off like a bird over the front fence and into that splendid, cream, ever-green magnolia down by the gate. Saw the whole

11

thing from my front window. She's been with me ever since."

"But you couldn't see your front fence from those windows," said Joe. "Not with all those trees and bushes and junk that you've got growing everywhere."

"I'm talking about seven or eight years ago," said Mrs. Carpenter, "and what I can see from my own front windows is entirely my business." She bent down and patted Agnes. "No more than a young and innocent lamb, and on her way to the meatworks, weren't you, boy?" She continued to stroke the sheep's head. "I've trained her as a guard dog. Haven't done too bad, have I?" Chuckle, cackle. "She works a wonder on door-to-door salespersons, stray cats and dogs, nosey parkers like you two, and uninvited members of my family." Another chuckle. "Tell me again what you want? You, boy!" she ordered Joe and prodded him with her walking stick.

Joe told her.

"Well, well, well," said Mrs. Carpenter. "So this is what they do in school these days instead of teaching you how to read and write." Then she smiled for the first time. "However, I must admit I really do fancy the part about your doing something in return." She smacked her lips. "We can think of a whole heap of things these two will very soon be doing in return, can't we, Agnes? A mountain of things that need doing around this old place." Mrs. Carpenter chuckled happily.

12

"That was really only if we had time," said Joe quickly. This was not going quite the way they had planned it.

"Don't you worry yourselves about that," said Mrs. Carpenter. "There'll be plenty of time." She looked down at her sheep. "Won't there, Agnes? Maybe I was just a little too hasty in passing my opinion on modern education. It seems they may be training you for something useful after all. Now, shall we make a start exactly as we mean to go on? I shall show you the kitchen and you shall make us all a cup of tea. What school did you say you were from?"

"Saint Joseph's Convent," said Belinda.

"But it's not our fault," said Joe.

"And you two didn't know the meaning of Agnes? Lamb of God? My goodness gracious me. It seems the Holy Roman Church isn't doing much better than the education system."

2
Old Mrs. Carpenter's Pioneer Days

"It all sounds a bit odd to me," said Mrs. Walsh, Joe's mother. "I think I should just check with your teacher."

"It was her idea in the first place," said Joe.

"Must be the first idea of hers you've ever bought," said Mr. Walsh, Joe's father.

"Don't you go nicking anything from that old bird's house and give us all a bad name," said Eddie Walsh, Joe's brother. "And you'd be in trouble with the cops again."

"I think she's a very nice old lady. I'm going to help her. It's my duty," said Joe.

Joe's mother, father and older brother all looked at each other, raised their eyebrows, and shook their heads.

"I'm most unhappy with that Mrs. Robinson teaming you up with that dreadful Walsh boy," said Mrs. Wiggins, Belinda's mother. "It's not healthy and I must write to her."

"It's okay, Mum. I'll make sure he doesn't get up to anything he shouldn't. I think it's what people say, you know. It's that thing about giving a dog a bad name," said Belinda.

"No one in their right mind would call their dog Joe Walsh," said Mr. Wiggins. "Be a certain recipe for disaster." He shook his head. "So the old lady's got a pet sheep has she? Often wondered what went on behind that high fence and all those trees. A sheep, eh?"

"Yes," said Belinda, "it's called Agnes. It was a present from God."

"Just don't you forget, dear, that you're allergic to cats," said her mother. "I don't want you coming down again."

"It's a sheep, Mum. It's not a cat," said Belinda.

"I'm sure you must be allergic to them too, dear," said Mrs. Wiggins. "Now, hand me my writing pad."

"Old Robinson won't let us have a cassette recorder. I know she won't," said Belinda to Joe.

"We won't ask her then," said Joe.

"We can't just nick one," Belinda protested.

"I know how to get into the audiovisual room without a key," said Joe. "We'll just take one. It'll sure save all that writing." He looked at Belinda out of the corner of his eye. "Okay. If we get caught you can just blame me."

"I will," said Belinda, "and so will my mum."

"Old Robinson's always going on about us finding different ways to present our work and our findings. She'll be so pleased," said Joe. "I'd take Eddie's, me brother's, boom box but he keeps it chained to his bed and it's got a padlock and all."

"I'm not surprised," said Belinda.

"And Dad keeps his bolt cutters locked away. And I got these for when she makes us make her cups of tea." Joe dragged a paper bag from the inside of his jacket. "They're doughnuts. Better'n those cookies she gave us last time."

"Where'd you nick them?" Belinda asked.

Mrs. Carpenter was expecting them. Agnes was tethered to the lower branch of a delicate Japanese maple. At the sight of Joe she pawed enthusiastically at the ground like a mildly angry bull. "If you ask me, that stupid sheep doesn't have any idea in the wide world what sort of animal it's supposed to be," said Joe.

"I think she's rather sweet," said Belinda.

"I don't," said Joe.

They knocked and waited and shivered in the damp gloom of too many trees. They knocked again. "She's out. I think we should just go," said Belinda as they both peered in through the clearest of the stained, leadlight glass-door panes.

"Hah!" from behind them. Belinda and Joe jumped, taken by surprise.

"So that's your little game! Trying to break in, eh?" It was Mrs. Carpenter. "Just as I suspected. Thieving little devils." Then she smiled. "I was around at the back of the house sorting out some

16

of the gardening and cleaning up you'll soon be doing for me. I had to sack my last gardener, a dear boy called Julian. So handsome, he was." She smiled again. "Forever busy with some strange plants instead of my garden. Agnes ate one once and she was strange for a week. She kept on mooing. Anyway, come inside," she ordered, leading the way.

The dark of the inside matched the green gloom of the outside. Furniture crammed the hallways and sitting rooms. There were old carpets and rugs, with heavy drapes of velvet and brocade keeping out what little light might otherwise have crept in from the jungle outside.

"You've brought a cassette recorder? Too lazy to write, eh?" said Mrs. Carpenter.

"You know what it is?" Belinda, surprised, nodded towards the recorder.

"What on earth did you think I'd think it was? A little magic what-not that talks? I may be old, child, but . . ." She did not continue for a moment but looked between her two visitors. A faint trace of a smile played at her lips. "You'd never believe it, but I've also got one of those other little boxes. You know the sort? What d'you call them? The ones with the pictures that come on with all the little people? What is it? Oh, what's it called? Silly old me . . ." She continued to smile.

"I think you might mean a television, Mrs. Carpenter," said Belinda patiently.

"Ah, yes. Now you mention it, maybe that's

what I do mean. My, what a wonderful invention it is. I've always wondered how they manage to stuff all those tiny wee people in at the back," said Mrs. Carpenter.

Belinda and Joe looked at each other as the old woman talked. They said nothing.

"One day I'm going to open up the back of my one and have a look. If only I could lay my hands on a screwdriver, I'd have something to poke around with." Mrs. Carpenter was smiling more widely.

"What sort of programs do you like, Mrs. Carpenter?" Belinda asked.

"Starting our interview already, are we? Me? What do I like?" She considered the question briefly. "Oh, I think . . . give me a nice juicy murder any day of the week. Nothing nicer than some of those wonderful videos you rent at the little video shop just past the bakery. I think my favorite one was about a young gentleman from Texas who took a chainsaw to most of his friends, some of his family and quite a few nosy visitors. You've seen it? Oh, it's a fine piece of work and an absolute gem of filmic art. Goodness knows how they do it. I must have seen it four times and I'd really love to get myself a good chainsaw."

"You're pulling our legs, eh?" said Joe.

"Bless you, child." Mrs. Carpenter looked surprised. "Why on earth would anyone want to pull your legs? Now then. Why don't we start with a nice cup of tea?"

"I got something for us to eat," said Joe, producing his bag of doughnuts.

"My word! You've brought a plate. How civilized," said Mrs. Carpenter.

"Nope, didn't bring no plate. Just the doughnuts. They're in a paper bag," said Joe.

"Agnes will love them," said Mrs. Carpenter, "and we three will have a piece of shortbread each. Much better for our digestion, I feel sure."

"Why on earth didn't I think to put you two to work together before?" said Mrs. Robinson, beaming at Belinda and Joe. "No one else in the whole, whole class has anything to report yet. We'd just love to listen to Belinda and Joe's interview with Mrs. Carpenter, wouldn't we class?" She smiled again. "What a splendid choice of elderly person. I wouldn't have thought that any of you in here would have known the old drag — old lady, I mean. It'll be wonderful indeed for us to hear about the early pioneer days almost from the horse's mouth. Turn it on Belinda. Nice and loud. Pay attention, everyone. Turn it up nice and loud so we all can hear it."

Crackle, crackle, crackle. *"Oh, hell,"* said the cassette player. Crackle, crackle. *"Testing, testing, one, two, three . . ."*

"Here. Give me a go, boy. I know how these things work even though you think I shouldn't, and after all, it's my words you want to record. Testing, testing. The

black cat sat on the mat." The voice of Mrs. Carpenter came from the machine.

Giggles.

"Testing, testing . . . the white cat sat on the mat." Belinda's voice and a few more giggles.

Laughs.

"Why do you let your sheep Agnes inside, Mrs. Carpenter? She goes all over your carpets and mats, eh?" Joe's voice.

Loud laughs from all the class.

"Does this last?" asked Mrs. Robinson.

"Have you ever tried to housetrain a sheep?" Mrs. Carpenter's voice. *"And if I don't mind her droppings, why should you? They're my carpets. Come on now. Fire away with those questions."*

The tape stopped. Sounds erupted from the recorder. One or two more words were spoken. More sounds . . . munching sounds. Then silence.

"Agnes the sheep started to eat the cord just about at this bit," explained Belinda to Mrs. Robinson and the class. "Mrs. Carpenter made us bring her in from outside for her doughnut and we had to tie her up to a chair. I'll just fast forward a bit." The interview finally got underway.

"Mrs. Carpenter, we please want to know what was life like in the olden days when you were a girl and a young woman?" Belinda's voice.

"Which?"

"Which what?"

"Those were the days. Ah, me. Those were the days." Mrs. Carpenter's voice.

Silence on the tape. "She's just thinking during this bit," Joe told the class.

"She's sure thinking for a long time," said one of their listeners. "Has she gone to sleep?"

"Or Joe Walsh knocked her out so he could nick things," said another. "He's like that."

"No. You just wait," said Belinda.

"The 1920s . . ." and another long silence. *"Yes, indeed. Those really were the days . . ."*

"Now we're getting there," said Mrs. Robinson expectantly. "This is it. Make sure you all listen carefully and write some notes," she said to her class. "Unpaved, muddy streets and all the brave young soldiers coming back from World War One. The old band rotunda down by the gardens and everyone churning butter by hand. Wonderful!"

Mrs. Carpenter's voice broke in. *"It was Paris — Paris, France. The City of Light. Dear, dear Paris and in my early twenties. Living on the left bank of the River Seine with the most wonderful artist you could ever imagine. Alphonse! My dear Alphonse. Where are you now, Alphonse? Dead, I'll be bound. Dead and buried, I imagine, the way you drank. Alphonse! He painted me, you know."*

"What color?" Joe's voice.

"All over?" Belinda.

"Not a stitch on me." Mrs. Carpenter's voice. *"My goodness me, did I have a figure then! Black hair halfway down my back. As black as yours, girl. Which reminds me. You're not Italian, are you?"*

"Part Maori." Belinda's voice.

21

"Which part?" Joe's voice.

"Is this my interview or is it not?" Mrs. Carpenter's voice, sounding slightly annoyed. "Do you, or do you not, want me to go on? Ah, yes, and that time he had me pose; a red rose between my teeth and a cigarette in a long, long ivory holder . . ." Pause.

"What else?" Belinda's voice.

"Nothing else, girl. Nothing at all."

"Be a bit hard knowing which one to smoke." Joe sniggered. "Could've been a bit cold too, eh?"

"Oh, those parties! The red wine flowing like water and everyone smoking . . ."

At this point there was a loud recorded crash and the machine seemed to go dead.

"It's Agnes the sheep, eh? Agnes knocked the table over trying to get another doughnut," said Joe to Mrs. Robinson and the class.

"Thank the Lord for small mercies," breathed Mrs. Robinson.

"Hey, come on. Get it going again. This is real good," said someone in the class. "Old Walsh and Wiggins done some work at last, eh, Mrs. Robinson?"

"Doesn't come back on," said Belinda. "When the sheep got into it, it all spewed out and when Mrs. Carpenter wound it all back on with her knitting needle it was okay to play the bit we recorded but it just wouldn't record anymore."

"Whoever would have thought . . . ? That sweet little elderly lady . . ." Mrs. Robinson wiped her forehead.

"Mrs. Carpenter said if she knew our school could only afford these cheap crap machines for recording she'd have hired us one to do a decent job," said Belinda. "From a nice guy she knows who gives her under-the-counter videos."

"She's going to do that anyway," said Joe. "We're going back tomorrow with a new tape and she's going to tell us the next bit. Great, eh?" He smiled at all the class. "I always thought the olden days must have been boring as anything. But not old Mrs. Carpenter's. After Alphonse painted her she got hung in a picture shop in the front window."

"They hung her?" someone called out. "They really hung her? How come if they hung her she's still here today?"

"Not that sort of hung, stupid. Her picture got hung up," Joe explained.

Belinda took over. "Mrs. Carpenter took off then, to some place called Sweden. She wanted what she called a natural life and that's the place to get it because it's the land of the midnight sun. It's daytime just about forever. She got out this old atlas and it's all marked where she's been and she's going to read us her diaries about what she did." Belinda turned to their teacher. "She sure didn't get round to churning any butter, Mrs. Robinson. I don't think there's any butter at all in Mrs. Carpenter's stories."

"No, but she met Hitler," said Joe.

"Hitler? I should've known," sighed Mrs. Robinson.

23

"Who's Hitler?" someone asked.

"You'll just have to wait and see and find out all about him. I think Mrs. Carpenter said that Hitler was some other sort of painter," said Belinda.

"Gee! Did he paint her, too?"

"And Mrs. Carpenter's going to get Joe and me to climb up in the attic of her house and get down all those boxes of photos and old stuff of what it was like in the olden days. She says if the mice haven't eaten it all we can pick out a whole heap and bring 'em along to school for a display. Good one, eh?"

"Has she still got the one of her and the red rose and nothing else?" asked another.

"I asked her that," said Joe, "but she can't remember. I thought it might be interesting for us to see what a today's old person looked like back then. Anyway, she said it didn't matter if that one was there or not because there were hundreds more quite like it. The ones I want to see are when she went to America and was a human cannonball. She was in a circus and she got to know all these crooks and gangsters and had parties with them. I just wish I'd been around in them days. Those were the days, she reckoned. Just like you reckon, Mrs. Robinson." Joe looked at their teacher.

3
Old Mrs. Carpenter's Family and More of Her Pioneer Days

"You seem to be forever at that old lady's house," said Mrs. Walsh. "I do hope you're not taking anything that doesn't belong to you, Joe. Not from a sweet little old lady."

"Course he is, Mum. Nicking things is why he goes there," said Eddie Walsh.

"I like Mrs. Carpenter," said Joe, "she's good. Real good. But not her shortbread. And she said to us, if she was going to help me and Belinda Wiggins out we had to help her out too."

"Yeah," sneered Eddie, "reckon she didn't mean help yourself though."

"We've raked up all her leaves from winter and Belinda's chopped back some old branches on the trees," said Joe, "and I helped George the bottle man move all her bottles."

"Milk bottles, dear?" asked his mother.

"That'll be the day," said Joe. "We help look after Agnes, her sheep, too. She's getting old now.

Mrs. Carpenter says she's getting arthritis."

"Poor old lady," said Mrs. Walsh. "Still, she is nearly ninety — or so I'm told."

"Yeah. They've both got it," said Joe. "Her and her sheep. She says it's the damp air in this town and people should be paid to live here and she doesn't know why she's bothered to stay so long and it's time the whole stinking place was bull-dozed."

"I'll sit down and write her a line just to make sure it's all right," said Mrs. Wiggins. "She's a very old lady and I don't like the thought of you tiring her out. And I must do her a kindness and let her know all about that dreadful Joe Walsh. It's not nice at all."

"There's not much wrong with Joe Walsh, Mum," said Belinda.

"That the father of a good hiding wouldn't fix," said her father, "and I'm just the man to give it to him."

"I must say I don't think it's healthy with that sheep living inside. You know we've got to watch your chest, Belinda," said her mother.

"Don't write to her, Mum. Please don't write," said Belinda. "You've got enough to do just writing to Mrs. Robinson all the time. The other kids laugh because she says things about your letters."

"Says things? Says things! What sort of things? What does she say? How dare she say anything." Mrs. Wiggins pursed her lips into a thin, tight line.

"Just tell me, Belinda, what sort of things does she say? Pass me my pad, dear."

In Mrs. Carpenter's garden they raked the leaves from the previous winter and autumn — and from many an autumn and winter before that. They even found one or two interesting plants that Mrs. Carpenter's last gardener, Julian, had left behind. Mrs. Carpenter took them inside for safekeeping. Joe set fire to the dampened pile of raked-up leaves and the smoke choked them all. It also had a most unpleasant effect on the customers and staff of the Food Giant Supermarket right next door.

"I shall burn whatever I choose, young man. I will burn it whenever I choose and wherever I choose," Mrs. Carpenter said to Garry, the young manager of the Food Giant, as they glared at each other through smoke-reddened and watery eyes, "and if anyone had ever told me when I gave my land on which your premises stand that one day I'd have a grocery shop right on my doorstep . . . well! The smoke, young man, is less from my leaves and more, much more, from the sacks of accumulated litter and trash blown into my property from your dreadful little shop."

Joe and Belinda trimmed the overgrowth of branches and cleared the undergrowth of weeds that the almost toothless Agnes chose to ignore as possible food.

"I think we're a bit mad," said Belinda.

"Why?" asked Joe.

"This'd cost old Mrs. Carpenter a fortune if she had to pay someone to do it. She should never have sacked that nice Julian."

"It's not much to do for an old lady," said Joe. "We haven't done that much."

"*You* haven't and that's for sure," said Belinda.

They met Mrs. Carpenter's only family that day. Her great-nephew Derek, Moira his wife, and their only child Shane called to see the old lady.

"Garry at the Food Giant called me, Aunty," said Derek. "He said how all that smoke is just about driving him mad and his trade's down nearly thirty percent on last week and it's hard times for us all."

"Dreadful little man. Shouldn't charge so much in the first place. Call you, indeed . . . Agnes! Leave that child alone," Mrs. Carpenter called out to her pet. Shane was flat on his back while Agnes, one foot planted on his chest, breathed into his face. Shane whimpered.

"Aunty! Do call that wretched creature off poor Shaney. Please dear," said Moira, Shane's mother.

"Belinda! Rescue the boy, there's a good girl," said Mrs. Carpenter, shaking her head. "As if he wasn't big enough — and quite ugly enough — to rescue himself."

"Who is Belinda?" asked Moira.

"One of my two new young friends. This is the other, Joe. A great help, both of them," said Mrs. Carpenter.

"Really, Aunty," said Moira. "Do you think it's wise opening up your home and property to absolute strangers?" She lowered her voice only slightly. "They could rob you blind and they probably will. One hears such dreadful things these days."

"As I was saying, Moira, when you rudely interrupted me, they are proving a great, great help. That's more, much more, than can be said for others I know and who should be offering to do more but most certainly do not." Mrs. Carpenter glared at Shane. "D'you know my two new friends, boy? You all seem to be about at the same age and ghastly stage of development."

"Yeah. No. I dunno," said Shane, clinging to his mother. "Yeah. I do know that one," he said pointing at Joe. "He's Joe-something and he's the one who nicks things. Don't go to my school, though."

"Nicks things?" asked Moira. "What do you mean, sweetheart?"

"Nuthin'," said Shane, looking at Joe.

"You've got to get rid of that wretched sheep, Aunty," said Derek. "Every time it sets eyes on our poor Shane . . . you gotta get rid of it. It's a menace."

"Get rid? Get rid! Get rid of it, Derek?" said Mrs. Carpenter. "What in heaven's name do you mean by that, boy?"

"It's a menace," Moira said, backing up her husband.

"And I hate its guts," said Shane rather quietly. "She's a cow, that sheep."

Mrs. Carpenter drew herself up to her full height, which made her somewhat taller than anyone else there. "Tell me, pray, if you can, which I doubt, just how you think I could rest easy in my bed at night — one old, defenseless lady, all alone, and we certainly know what that means in these evil times as you've just pointed out to me, Moira — without my good Agnes to keep an eye on things? Oh dear me no. My faithful Agnes has many a long year left in her yet."

Derek, Moira and Shane eyed Agnes up and down and there was no kindness in their six eyes. They edged carefully past the sheep and followed the old lady inside.

"Don't reckon Agnes got too many years left in her if they have anything to do with it," Joe said to Belinda.

"Don't be horrible," said Belinda. "She's just about the nicest old sheep anyone could hope for and I'm positive no one would harm a hair on her head."

"She's a right pain of a sheep and you know it," said Joe. "She's a right pain of a sheep and I've felt it." Joe rubbed his backside. "As a sheep, Agnes just does not know her place at all."

"What is her place?"

"A sheep's place is in a paddock," said Joe firmly. "Then it's in a freezer. Then on your plate. Or, it's in a paddock and then in a bale of wool and then you wear it. If you ask me, a sheep's place is not in an old lady's garden on Gladstone Road."

"Yeah, well, that just proves how dumb you are and how clever Agnes is. A very cunning and clever sheep of God is Mrs. Carpenter's Agnes." Belinda looked at the animal. "I wonder if she might have some lambs? She sure looks big enough and I'd like a pet lamb."

It was not often that Derek, Moira and their son Shane called on Derek's great-aunt. The only thing the three of them had in common with Mrs. Carpenter was that they came from the same family. "You can scarcely blame me for that," the old woman told Belinda and Joe.

"Why not?" asked Joe.

"Derek is the son of my sister's daughter," said Mrs. Carpenter.

"So where's your sister then?"

"My sister Phoebe is dead. So is her daughter, Veronica. It was a great tragedy." Mrs. Carpenter did not explain. "Derek is my only living flesh and blood and that is a cross I must bravely bear."

"So is Shane," said Belinda.

"Who?" asked Mrs. Carpenter. "Before my sister died — such a silly thing she was — I made the promise to her that, one day," Mrs. Carpenter said, waving her hands about, "all this would go to Derek. She brought him up you know. As I often told her, she did not make a very good job of it."

"You mean when you die, that Derek gets your house and everything?" said Joe.

"That's right."

"And Agnes?" Belinda asked.

"Well, I can't take a sheep with me girl," said Mrs. Carpenter sharply. "Besides, as I've already told you, I am charging you with the care of Agnes. Why on earth else do you think I'm taking all this time and trouble with the two of you?"

"I thought you liked our company," said Joe. He looked around. "And our work in your garden."

"That's as may be," said Mrs. Carpenter. "Now get busy clearing out that corner over there," she pointed, "and when that's done we'll have a cup of tea. Did you bring any of those nice doughnuts, boy? I'm getting quite a taste for them. I'll have the doughnuts and you can have the shortbread."

Belinda and Joe continued to visit Mrs. Carpenter. Sometimes they called once a week, sometimes once a fortnight. Usually it was on a Saturday. Away from Mrs. Carpenter's place they had no contact with each other. Joe had his friends, Belinda had hers. At school their paths did not cross. The study of the needs and memories of the local elderly was soon a thing of the past. Mind you, some aspects of it were long remembered.

Mrs. Robinson borrowed a butter churn from the Early Settlers' Museum and managed to find someone who had once made butter by hand. The class enjoyed a demonstration and soon the room was awash in cream. Mrs. Robinson also managed to wriggle out of retirement a very old farmer who owned a very old draught horse and who had an even older tree stump out in a paddock. The whole class went out for a demonstration. At first, the horse did not want to be caught, and then refused to be harnessed. The old farmer said, "Damn fool thing to want to see anyway," to Mrs. Robinson and, "Cedric! Go and get the bloody tractor. That'll fix the sod," to his son and, "You'll be dog meat next week, mark my words!" to the horse, after which the whole of Mrs. Robinson's class took turns having rides around the paddock on the motorized, four-wheel farm bikes before heavy rain drove them back to school early.

Mrs. Carpenter's second and last interview was a great success. Her friendship with the young Adolf Hitler in Germany had lasted only for a weekend and it was thought to be a good idea for her to leave that country quite quickly. Adolf had not enjoyed being called a homicidal maniac in the making and a menace to the future of the human race. So, off to Chicago in the United States of America where she began a short career as a human cannonball in a circus.

"Ah, the days of prohibition. Wonderful! Wonderful! Wonderful!" Mrs. Carpenter's voice.

"What's prohibition?" Belinda's voice.

"Don't they teach you anything at all at that school of yours?" Mrs. Carpenter's voice.

"Not much." Joe's voice. "Saint Joseph's has great trouble getting the services of decent teachers. That's what our priest said at Mass last Sunday."

"Doesn't surprise me at all if you two are an example of what the poor souls have to put up with!" Mrs. Carpenter's voice.

"Right on!" said Mrs. Robinson to the cassette recorder.

"Prohibition was probably the most exciting period in the whole of the history of the United States of America. At least as far as I was personally concerned. Prohibition meant no booze. Not one drop. Booze was illegal. Ah, me. How thrilling it all was," the old lady sighed.

"Doesn't sound exciting." Belinda's voice. "That'd just about drive my dad mad."

"It might well have been illegal but the whole country was afloat in an ocean of the stuff. Smuggled in, it was, from north of the border. From Canada. You've heard of Canada? No?" Mrs. Carpenter's voice.

"I don't think this very interesting interview has much to do with growing up in the olden days," said Mrs. Robinson. "Joe? Belinda? Maybe we could just leave it there. Such a good effort from the two of you."

But no one heard Mrs. Robinson because Joe turned up the volume on the recorder and all that could be heard was Mrs. Carpenter talking about her deep and meaningful relationship with a man called Marco who owned a fleet of trucks that brought in the oceans of illegal booze from Canada. A friendship that would have lasted a lifetime had

34

not another guy, Manfredo, machine-gunned Marco, who had once been his best friend, in a delicatessen shop and in his prime. All of this meant that old Mrs. Carpenter only had time for another couple of shots out of her cannon so that she could collect her week's wages and her danger money before racing halfway across the United States of America in a bulletproof car and jumping on a steamship home to the South Pacific and safety.

"You know what?" Belinda asked of the class.

"What?" Mrs. Robinson shuddered.

"She's been here ever since," said Belinda. "She said she'd had enough excitement to last three lifetimes and it was time for a bit of absolute boredom."

"Thank the good Lord," said Mrs. Robinson.

"Her old man, her father, he died soon after she got back and she inherited his house and all the land around it, even where our school is now. She's just sold off bits of it when she's needed more money for the thieving tax man and the rates. She married Mr. Carpenter and he was devoted to her, hand and foot, for the whole of the rest of his life until the day he died even though he was the most dead-boring man ever invented," Belinda finished.

"I suppose he would seem a wee bit boring," said Mrs. Robinson, "after Hitler and Alphonse and Mr. Marco in Chicago. Remarkable!" She shook her head and spoke softly to herself.

35

"Whoever would have thought it of the old girl? I really must borrow that tape for a couple of nights."

"Sheep are a vastly underrated animal," said Mrs. Carpenter. "Man has much to learn from them."

"Like what?" asked Joe.

"Like intelligence," said Mrs. Carpenter. "My observation of this old girl, old Agnes, convinces me of that. A creature of high intelligence. She's a Border Leicester Romney Cross, you know."

"How d'you know that?" asked Belinda.

"A farmer told me. They live a long time. That's if man gives them half a chance," said Mrs. Carpenter.

"They don't often live as long as Agnes," said Belinda. "It's a pity about her teeth."

"Nothing wrong with her teeth," said the old woman, "she just hasn't got any."

"You should get her false teeth," said Joe. "My mum's got some false teeth. Someone left them at one of our parties. She says she's saving them for later, for when she's old and might need them."

"Very wise," said Mrs. Carpenter.

"I could bring 'em down and try 'em out on old Agnes first, eh?" Joe offered.

"It's very kind of you, boy, but you'll do no such thing," said Mrs. Carpenter.

"She'd choke," said Belinda.

"A sheep does not need false teeth." Mrs. Carpenter looked at them. "Just remember, stale bread, a sprinkling of sugar and half a bottle of milk. You should warm the milk in winter to take the chill off. And don't forget some chopped up cabbage, just lightly steamed. Say once or twice a week? It's for her regularity."

"For her what?"

"To make her bowels move, girl. The bread and milk does tend to stop her up a bit after a while. That's all there is to it. A simple task. You'll find her no trouble at all."

"What about shearing?" asked Joe.

"There's the two of you. Let common sense prevail. By all means share the burden. Not that one sheep could be counted any burden at all."

"No," said Joe, "*shear*. Like in cutting off her wool. She's sure got a lot of it."

Mrs. Carpenter looked at Agnes. "Oh, yes. Yes. It is about time for her next haircut. So hard to get a farmer willing to go a few rounds with the old girl. Why, last time . . ."

"There's enough wool on her now to pay for the bread and the milk for quite a while," said Joe softly.

"If you are saying you begrudge, young man . . ."

"We don't mind, Mrs. Carpenter," said Belinda quickly. "Not at all. We'll look after Agnes. Anyway, you're not going to die for years and years. Don't you worry." She kicked Joe on the ankle.

Mrs. Carpenter stood. "You will not find Agnes and me ungrateful," she said.

"Eh?" said Joe.

"Pick up her bowl, boy," she said, pointing to Agnes's blue and white bowl. "Give it to me." She took it from his hand. "You know what this is?" she asked sharply.

"An old bowl," said Joe.

"Right. There are several of them," said Mrs. Carpenter. "Quite a few, in fact."

"We won't run out of bowls for Agnes then," said Belinda.

"I intend taking these bits and pieces to my lawyer, Mr. Claude Cotter of Cotter, Cotter and Partners, very soon. You've heard of them?" Mrs. Carpenter asked.

"No," said Joe "why?"

"No matter," said Mrs. Carpenter. "They are called Ming and Ching."

"Who, the lawyers?" asked Belinda.

"Why do I bother?" Mrs. Carpenter shook her head. "Let me say just this. Claude Cotter will have instructions. Look after Agnes when I croak and, when you're old enough, the Chinese porcelain will be yours. Go now. I'm tired."

"What was all that about the bowls?" Belinda asked Joe on their way home.

"I think the old girl's going off her rocker. Might be we go and see this Claude if Agnes breaks a bowl and we need another one. I dunno. Reckon all we need is a plastic bucket." He looked at Belinda. "Look, I don't want to look after any old vicious sheep. I don't. She better not die, old Mrs. Carpenter."

"She won't," said Belinda. "My mum says old ladies like that live just about forever."

"She should know," said Joe. "I reckon old Mrs. Carpenter is half off her nut."

"She's just old," said Belinda, "like you will be some day. That's if they let you live long enough."

"What's Ching and Ming, Mum?" Joe asked his mother as they ate dinner.

"No idea, Joe," said Mrs. Walsh.

"It's something to do with old plates," said Joe.

"No it's not," scoffed Eddie Walsh, "it's Kung Fu. That's what it is. Or karate. It's when they break up piles of plates. Real cool."

"For once in his lifetime your brother is right, Edward," said their father. "Ming and Ching *are* old plates. Old china from China. Very old. Worth a small fortune. Funny. I was just reading about it the other day."

"What you want to know for?" asked Joe's brother.

"None of your business," said Joe.

"Boys! Boys!" said Mrs. Walsh.

"Dad! Mum! I reckon Joe's nicked one. I reckon he's nicked one of them plates. I bet he has. Don't say I didn't warn you!"

4
The Late Mrs. Carpenter

When old Mrs. Carpenter died peacefully in her sleep it was the milkman who found her. He had been alerted by the loud and persistent bleating of Agnes calling for her morning helping of milk-soaked and sugared bread. Agnes was not used to being kept waiting. The milkman went to investigate.

It was to be two days before Agnes next plowed into her favorite food and during this time she had to make do with a sampling of the softer weeds and grasses, uncooked, that she scavenged from the half-tidied wilderness garden of her late owner.

Mrs. Carpenter's great-nephew Derek, the doctor, and the undertaker all arrived at the Gladstone Road house at much the same time. "There'll have to be an inquest," said the doctor. "She died at home."

"Hope it won't take too long," said Derek.

"God! What's that?" said the undertaker, spotting Agnes in the undergrowth.

"It's Aunty's sheep," said Derek.

"Could've fooled me," said the undertaker. "Looks like a yeti."

"Yeah, well, won't be looking like anything much in a day or two when I get round to it. That sheep's following Aunty double damn quick," said Derek.

The doctor and the undertaker looked at Derek sideways. "Shall we discuss the casket?" said the undertaker. "There's some lovely wood around these days, really lovely, and she was a very well-known citizen and pioneer of our town. A grand old lady." He had never met her but had heard stories.

"Nothing too fancy," said Derek. "Aunty didn't have too much to come and go on, moneywise, and she wouldn't like the thought of what little she did have being wasted on fancy coffins. Something simple would be nicest."

Again the doctor and the undertaker looked sideways at each other, then at Derek. This time they raised their eyebrows too. The magnitude of the late Mrs. Carpenter's fortune and property was as well known as she had been. "Burial or cremation?" asked the undertaker. "What would the old lady have liked?"

"How much do they cost?" asked Derek as they came out onto the verandah of the house, leaving the doctor inside to fill out one or two forms. Derek

41

looked around at what he knew was now all his. He breathed in deeply the damp and moldy air of the garden. "All this will soon be gone," he said almost to himself.

"None of us can live forever," said the undertaker, mistaking what Derek had said and laying a comforting hand on the other's shoulder. "She was an old, old lady."

"It's all going to be a parking lot," said Derek.

"Er . . . um . . ." said the undertaker, sorting out in his mind something right to say. "Earth to earth. Ashes to ashes," he murmured as they walked down the steps into the gloom of the garden.

In his great grief Derek had forgotten the presence of Agnes. Like a cannonball Agnes rocketed from her haven in the undergrowth, a vast, woolly projectile, and took Derek at the knees. Heavier than his son Shane, he did not travel quite so far or so fast. However, he certainly travelled louder. One high-pitched yell, more squeal than scream, and Derek did major damage to a rather nice, late-blooming camellia. Satisfied, Agnes ambled back into the shrubbery from where she eyed him angrily. The undertaker came down from the verandah and the doctor from the house. Both did their very best to extricate their client from the greenery.

"She's mutton," Derek muttered, "mutton. She's mutton!"

* * *

The late Mrs. Carpenter's funeral, a simple but dignified affair, was held at St. David's Presbyterian Church right across the road from St. Joseph's Convent School. It was attended by many. The end of an era. "A great old girl," the mayor was heard to murmur as he and almost all the other mourners hung around the church after the service. There was nowhere else for them to go, other than their own homes. Derek and Moira had decided against putting on afternoon tea and a drink for those who had turned up to pay their last respects.

"It's not as if Aunty was close to anyone. We didn't really think that anyone would expect it of us," Derek said to the mayor.

"And I've never thought that entertaining after a funeral was in very good taste," said Moira. "After all, it's not a rugby match. And, of course, we're all so upset at Aunty's sudden passing. Grief, you know, attacks different people in different ways," she finished.

"Attacks some I know right square in the pocket," said the doctor to the mayor after Derek and Moira had moved on to whisper sadly in the ears of another cluster of mourners.

"Is that all there is?" said Joe to Belinda.

"Yeah. I think it is. Mum says Presbyterians aren't like us micks, eh? When our Uncle Brian O'Flaherty died we had this party and it went on for a week," said Belinda. "Still be going on probably but Mum finally had had enough, said she'd

43

bury anyone with her own hands if they didn't get out of her house and off to their own houses double-quick."

In view of their close connection to the deceased, Mrs. Robinson had allowed Joe and Belinda to attend the church service. Indeed, most of Mrs. Robinson's class had suddenly found close connections, one way or another, to the late Mrs. Carpenter. Mrs. Robinson had felt quite happy to dispatch a fairly large proportion of her class. The function itself proved a significant disappointment to most of them.

Joe and Belinda had made no secret of the fact that their inside information on the late old lady indicated that the funeral would likely be attended by quite a few elderly figures, old friends from the late Mrs. Carpenter's days in Chicago, Sweden and Paris. They had even heard that Adolf Hitler from Germany was going to turn up or, at the very least, send a recorded message, and that the full-length nude portrait of the late Mrs. Carpenter painted by her pal Alphonse was going to be on display at the head of her coffin. One or two of Mrs. Robinson's class had even been persuaded by Joe that the late Mrs. Carpenter's coffin and all would be sped on its way to heaven from a gigantic cannon that was to be set up in the gardens of the Presbyterian Church. After all, wasn't that the only way that Presbyterians were likely to get into heaven?

It was a letdown in more ways than one for most

who attended. "Well, she was right," said Belinda. "She's gone now."

"You only just noticed," said Joe. "The hearse drove off ten minutes ago."

"What about Agnes?"

"She didn't go," said Joe. "Not that I could see."

"You're a pain. You certainly are a pain. Look. We got this agreement. We've got to look after Agnes now. Whether we like it or not. We've just got to do it. It's just . . ." Belinda shook her head. "I don't know how."

Joe fully agreed with her. "I know," he said. "And I found out about Ming and Ching."

"So did I," said Belinda. "Mum says they're museum pieces."

"Let's go and get some bread and some milk," said Joe. "May as well get started."

"And let's start thinking about what to do with that old sheep," said Belinda.

"I know what I'd like to do with it," said Joe.

Belinda looked at him. "Yeah, I know. Still, we can't, eh?" She went on looking at him. "We just can't."

"No. I know that," said Joe. "We gotta look after that bloody old sheep." He looked up at the sky. "It's for her sake. I reckon she is somewhere up there."

"Yes," said Belinda, "and if you ask me, I reckon she's laughing right down at us. Come on."

5

The Almost Late Agnes

"I simply cannot understand where all the bread's going these days," said Mrs. Walsh, Joe's mother. "Seems we're getting through more than two whole loaves a day."

"Hollow legs on those boys, that's what it is," said her husband.

"And milk! They're drinking it like it's going out of fashion. You'll simply have to give me more for housekeeping, Fred, if they keep going at this rate," said Mrs. Walsh.

"Can't give you what I haven't got, dear," Mr. Walsh said reasonably. "They're growing boys you know."

"That's as may be. As I see it, one night less a week at the club for their old man might have to be on the cards. They're your sons, too."

"Are you sure?" said Mr. Walsh miserably.

The first week was easy. The late Mrs. Carpenter's house stood locked and deserted. The only sign of life as Joe and Belinda climbed the back

46

fence at a corner well hidden from prying eyes would be a rapid scuttling in the undergrowth. A hungry Agnes impatient for her bread, milk or part-cooked cabbage would emerge. There was no way they could heat the food but the old sheep did not seem to mind and would demolish with great enthusiasm whatever they had brought.

"D'you reckon her great-nephew Derek has forgotten about Agnes?" Belinda asked Joe.

"I doubt it," said Joe. "If you ask me, I reckon that Derek and his missus and that kid of theirs — and I'd love to thump that one — were just waiting for Mrs. Carpenter to kick the bucket. Anyway, that's what she told me one day."

"She did not," said Belinda. "I think Mr. Claude Cotter, of Cotter, Cotter and Partners, might have told them they've got to wait. I do think it could be possible he might have forgotten it's now all his." She looked hopeful.

"You gotta get the bread next week," said Joe. "Mum's going mad at what she says I'm eating."

"Couldn't you just nick some?" Belinda asked nicely.

"I can't tell her we're feeding it to a sheep," said Joe. "She'd just never believe me."

"There's that cake shop," said Belinda, pouring more milk into Agnes's plastic bucket, "that one down by the bus stop. It has all its cakes out on the counter. You could easily nick some from there. If we can't get Agnes any bread we could feed her some cake."

"Mum says the Food Giant dumps all its old and stale bread on Saturday mornings and it's real cheap. She says that's what we gotta have from now on. I just think you and me might have to buy some of that for old Agnes. You and me," he added meaningfully. Joe looked unhappily at Agnes. "How long d'you think she'll live for?" he asked. "I don't think she's missing Mrs. Carpenter at all."

"The way she eats, well, I'd reckon another eight or nine years," said Belinda quite happily. "I hope so anyway. She's a right healthy sheep."

"I can't spend the next eight or nine years of my life looking after an old sheep," said Joe. "I'd be grown up by then."

"Yeah. And in jail," said Belinda.

The real difficulties of looking after an elderly sheep did not begin for the two of them until well into the second week.

Derek and Moira had not forgotten that they now owned the late Mrs. Carpenter's house, contents and land. Neither had they forgotten they owned Agnes. It was Agnes they looked down upon one afternoon from the safety of the house verandah. "What are we going to do about that poor animal?" asked Moira.

"Calling in to see George this afternoon. She might be old but she should be good for a freezer full of sausages. Might be worth a buck or two," said Derek.

"Yes," said Moira, "it'd be a kindness really. You can see how she misses the old lady." Agnes pawed the ground and kept a close eye on Shane who stood between his parents. "And we are low on sausages," Moira added.

"You gonna get it killed, Dad?" Shane's eyes lit up and a broad grin spread across his face. "Good!" he breathed happily.

"Don't be horrible and nasty, darling," said Moira. "It's only a poor, dumb animal."

"Soon be a wasted dumb animal," said Shane. "Pee-ow!" he pointed a pistolled finger at Agnes. "Blow you away sheep," and he grinned again.

George the butcher was less than enthusiastic at being offered Agnes. "Last thing I need, Derek, is another sheep," he said pointing to a line of halved or quartered and quite dead sheep that hung from hooks along the back wall of his shop. "Dime a dozen these days. I'll turn one of these into sausages for you. Great condition too." He pinched the meat on the leg of the sheep hanging nearest him. "Still," he winked at Derek and rubbed his thumb against his forefinger, "make it worth my while and I'll take anything off your hands."

From the starting point of making a buck or two from Agnes, Derek had moved to the idea of maybe giving her away. He had not as yet moved so far as to consider paying anyone to take the old beast off his hands.

Kevin, the butcher's apprentice, saved Derek's bacon. Or mutton. "Maybe I could take it for you,

Mr. Pike," he said, and then blushed red to the roots of his head of fair hair. Kevin was not in the habit of saying very much at all.

"You?" said George his boss, surprised at Kevin's opening his mouth and actually speaking. "Not enough meat in here for you already? Gawd alive!"

Kevin summoned up all his courage. "Me mate Bruce and me, we got these two pig dogs we just bought and they sure as eggs take some feeding. Keeping 'em in chow sure costs a real heap. That's if you want it done, Mr. Pike," he said to Derek very politely and wishing for all he was worth that he had not opened his mouth in the first place.

Derek breathed a sigh of great relief and also upped his getting-rid-of-Agnes money prospects. "Come round after you've finished work, kid. Make me an offer. You know where the old girl lived?"

Derek and Shane, Kevin, Belinda and Joe arrived at the late Mrs. Carpenter's place at roughly the same time, although not with identical purpose. The conversation of the first three struck horror into the hearts and heads of the other two as they hid easily out of view behind a magnolia tree and a couple of rhododendrons.

Agnes, quite unconcerned, waited patiently, alert, ready for food and to take her pleasure with Shane who, as always, clung to the verandah.

"Aw, dunno Mr. Pike." Kevin shook his head

as he patted Agnes's. Agnes licked the hand that possibly would kill her. "Didn't know this was what you meant." Kevin looked slyly at Derek. Shy he most certainly was but the apprentice butcher was no one's fool. He had spotted early on that Agnes was a burden Derek found hard to bear. Agnes was also a load that Kevin, now he had seen her, most definitely wanted to shoulder. That pelt! That wool! All that long, matted, filthy, and bedraggled wool was a sight for sore eyes. Agnes was wearing the most wonderful coat of wool that Kevin in all his eighteen years had ever seen. Take that wonderful coat off the old sheep, cure it, tan it, brush and comb it and what more splendid, perfect gift ever would he be able to come up with for his widowed mother Myra's fortieth birthday in a couple of months' time? Kevin was known as an excellent son.

Kevin shook his head again. "Dunno, Mr. Pike," he said softly.

"Tell you what, lad. She's yours. All yours. She's yours for the killing," said Derek generously. "Just want to get rid of her."

Kevin continued to shake his head, not believing what he was hearing. "Eh?" he said.

Derek misunderstood the signals and threw a lifetime of great caution to the winds. "Get rid of the old cow — sheep — and here's ten bucks besides. Just for your trouble that is," he said, fishing in his pocket.

A broad and happy smile spread right across

Kevin's face. "Okay, Mr. Pike," he said and held out his left hand. His right hand continued to stroke the head of his gift. "Can't take her now though, Mr. Pike. Only got me bike." He nodded towards the gate where his bike stood.

"When?" Derek was anxious.

" 'Bout an hour. Me mate Bruce won't be home till then. Need his pickup, see? We'll take her and do her in the shed down the back of his place." Kevin knew his mother would dislike the sight, the sound and the mess of his slaughtering an elderly sheep in their own backyard. Besides, there was really very little room in her neat garden of roses and small blue and yellow conifers.

Hidden, Joe and Belinda shivered. It was a cold afternoon and it seemed to be getting colder. They looked at each other and, without saying a word, moved slightly closer together in order to capture a bit of human warmth.

Shane, on the other hand, was ecstatic. Shane was joyful. "When you gonna do her, Kevin? When you gonna do her? When? When you gonna do her?"

"When me mate Bruce gets home," said Kevin simply. "Sometime. He's out in the bush doin' a job. Why?"

Shane breathed so heavily he was panting. "Can I help youse two? Eh, Kevin? Eh? Can I help youse? Please?"

"Don't reckon we need no help. Not just doin' one old sheep." Kevin was puzzled.

"Can I just come and watch then?" Shane's eyes danced, shone brightly.

"Sure, kid, if you want." Kevin shrugged his shoulders. "Be 'bout an hour Mr. Pike." He gave Agnes a last look and a last pat.

"Just so long as I get rid of it from here," said Derek.

Kevin headed off down the path. Belinda and Joe heard his footsteps, saw his legs through the foliage and looked at each other again. He had almost reached the front gate when Shane, over-heated at the thought of pleasures to come and somewhat forgetful of his circumstances, suddenly remembered he had no idea where Bruce, Kevin's best mate, lived. "Hey, Kev!" he yelled. Kevin did not turn. Shane took one jump from beside his father, made a nice and neat landing in a clump of daffodils and managed two or three steps towards the gate.

Shane's yell as Agnes hoisted him from the side and very high — much, much higher than she usually managed — could be heard in all corners of the supermarket carpark next door and even in parts of the Food Giant building itself.

Joe and Belinda each smiled a very small smile.

6
Agnes on the Run

Belinda looked at Joe. Joe looked at Belinda and said, "What now?"

"I dunno," said Belinda.

"Guess it solves our problem, eh?" said Joe, looking at Belinda out of the corner of his eye.

Belinda did not trouble herself to make the reply she knew he expected. "Where are we going to put her?"

"Who?" Joe asked stupidly.

"Your backyard? At least your mum'd find out who's eating all her bread."

"In our backyard?" asked Joe. "Are you serious? She wouldn't last any longer with my dad than she's going to last with that Kevin. What about Dad's spuds? What about his silverbeet and sprouts and all his carrots? What about your backyard?"

"Mum's allergic to wool," said Belinda firmly.

"She only wears man-made fibers and Agnes'd bring her out in a rash all over her body."

"Where then?" they said together and looked helplessly at each other.

"I know where we can put her just for now," said Belinda. "Until Sunday, that is."

"Where?"

"Behind our church. There's all that long grass there that Father McIntosh can't get anyone to cut down. There's trees too, just like she's got here. No one'd spot her and Father McIntosh is just so old he'd . . ."

Joe interrupted. "Yeah, and he's half blind. Well, he sure is when he drinks and that's most days . . ."

"He'd never spot her and that'd give us three, four days to sort out something permanent."

"Yeah, well, unless we get a move on, something permanent is just about to get sorted out for her."

They waited as long as they considered safe. Would Kevin, so keen to get his hands on the hide of Agnes, be back early? Would Kevin's best mate Bruce be held up in the bush longer than expected? Would Shane Pike, probably more keen than either Kevin or Bruce to see the blood of Agnes spout forth, turn up to partake in the transportation as well as the execution of the old sheep? Joe and Belinda waited until dusk fell. Then, with a combination of great difficulty and personal pain they transported Agnes as secretly as possible from the garden of the late Mrs. Carpenter to the grounds of St. Joseph's Catholic Church.

It is not easy to walk a very large sheep quietly and unobserved through the streets of a town. Quite likely it is easier with some sheep than with others. Agnes was definitely one of the others. After all, this was her first look outside the wrought-iron gates over which she had flown as a lamb some seven or eight years ago, a gift from Allied Farmers' Transport.

"Don't you understand, you dumb, thick sheep, that we're doing this, him and me, to save your life?" said Belinda slowly, through gritted and grating teeth. She picked herself up from out of the gutter where Agnes had playfully bunted her.

Joe held on for all he was worth to the short length of rope they had knotted around the animal's neck. Joe wished, as hard as he held, that the rope was a noose. Agnes absorbed every mite of his physical energy while he spent his mental energies working out their route through the quietest, least-populated streets of the town.

Of the odd trio, Agnes was the least concerned. During the course of the half-hour lug around back streets and deserted lots she managed to take out two letter boxes, three small shrubs, had eaten most of a quite nice, vivid yellow iris plant and had scared the pants off a pair of very young Boy Scouts on their way to the Scout Hall.

"It's a bear!" cried one and took off as fast as he could. "It's a wild bear!" he yelled over his shoulder.

"It's a unicorn. It's that unicorn thing and it's got one yellow horn," yelled the other following him. Agnes started after them. She was wearing one yellow iris in the wool of her forehead.

"I just wish Kev and his mate Bruce would find us," said Joe miserably. "I just do. I really do. We've done our very best." He looked up at the sky.

For once Belinda half agreed with him. "He's quite nice, that Kevin. Mum always gets our meat from him. She says he's a lovely boy and he's very good to his mother who's had a hard time." Then she realized what she was saying. "But he's a murderer and an evil-minded killer for all that. You should've seen the blood-red look in his eye when he spotted old Agnes. Poor old Agnes."

Poor old Agnes discovered it was very boring hiding away under a bush so she took the opportunity to yank herself free of Joe's grip and canter off down the middle of the road. It was impossible to tell how far her old legs would have carried her because as quickly as she had started she stopped. She saw, or smelled, or sensed, the presence of the milkman. More than likely she heard the familiar clink, chink and rattle of the milk bottles and knew exactly what this foretold.

Joe caught her. It wasn't hard — she was glued

to the spot. Agnes would not budge. Belinda whacked Agnes hard, then harder still across her rump. She would not move.

The milkman came nearer.

"We gotta do something," hissed Joe.

"I'll thump her again," said Belinda. It had no effect.

They were saved by a train. Approaching a nearby level crossing, the train engine let off a mighty hoot of its whistle. Agnes momentarily forgot the comforting promise of the milkman and his goods. She bolted, terrified and bewildered, onto the front verandah of a house that very much resembled that of her late owner.

"Is that the Jehovah's?" said an old voice from the inside of the house, mistaking the rat-tat-tat of Agnes's hooves for the door-knocker. "Is that the Jehovah's out there?"

"Yes," said Joe, hearing the voice as he grabbed at the sheep. "Yes," in a deeper voice, "I am the Jehovah!"

"We don't want any today, thank you very much," said the old voice.

"All right," said Joe, "we'll go then." He dragged a reluctant Agnes from the porch.

Finally, they made it to the grounds of St. Joseph's Catholic Church, tethered Agnes and then looked at each other. "That's all I'm gonna do today for that sheep. You live nearer here than me, Wiggins. You get her some bread and some milk. See ya tomorrow." Joe took off into the dark.

* * *

"How did she get away?" asked Kevin reasonably of Derek who, out of habit, stood on the verandah of his late great-aunt's house.

"Search me," Derek grinned. "I thought it was you who'd taken. it. Maybe she heard what you had in store for her," he grinned again.

Kevin was not grinning. Kevin was a most upset youth. He was puzzled. Where was his one-in-a-lifetime sheep? How had this prize managed to escape his good keen grasp? How? After all, he had bought it. Well, almost bought it. Bit hard to ask for your money back when the seller had actually paid you to take the goods in the first place.

Kevin was miserable. He had already hinted to his mum, Myra, that something good was going to come her way in the not-too-distant future and that the something good was going to feel like heaven to her arthritic feet. "Goodness, sweetheart, not another pair of fluffy slippers, surely? My little old curlyhead is just so good to his old mum," Myra had said as she ruffled his hair. "Go on, tell me. Mummy's boy tell his old mum?" But he would say no more. "You just spoil me rotten, you silly wee goose."

The silly wee goose and little old curlyhead scratched his head as he peered, puzzled, at Derek on the verandah. "That kid of yours wouldn't've . . . ?" he said, remembering the blood-lust light in Shane's eyes.

"Well . . ." Derek considered the possibility,

59

"guess he sure would've liked to but don't reckon he'd be able to. Not all by himself. Now, if you'll excuse me . . . got a truck coming in half an hour. Taking this junk to the dump." Derek nodded to a pile of the late Mrs. Carpenter's household property. He felt no need at all to assist Kevin further. After all, getting rid of Agnes had cost him ten bucks and as far as he was concerned the sheep had gone.

Derek turned again to his sifting and sorting and, while Kevin again searched the undergrowth of the garden, he heaved from the house another pile of tattered old floor rugs that were dotted all over with a liberal plastering of Agnes's droppings. The sooner they went to the dump the better.

Derek was not to know that in a week's time the old rugs would be unearthed and excavated from beneath mountains of rotting crud, spotted by the eagle eyes of Mrs. Carmen Sylvester, Chairperson of the Drama Society. She regularly scoured and scavenged and picked over the litter of the town for treasures with which to decorate the stage of the Little Theater for her upcoming play productions. Mrs. Carmen Sylvester thought she had won a lottery! A few weeks of painstaking unpeeling by hand of sheep manure from the ancient fabrics, a gentle lathering with baby shampoo and a slow dry in the shade, and Mrs. Sylvester had become the owner of a small fortune in rare and antique oriental rugs.

"She's sure not here," said Kevin to Derek, even

60

more miserably following his further futile and fruitless search of the garden.

"I told you that," said Derek. "Now, give us a hand to load this stuff onto the truck. After all, kid, I did pay you to get rid of the old sod and you didn't."

7
Agnes Tours Church, Farm and School

It was late that same afternoon that Father McIntosh connected with Agnes, as the sheep rested under the steps leading into the back entrance to the church. The priest had paused for a moment on the top step to admire the coming-into-leaf of a particularly lovely, young golden elm tree he had planted some years before in order to give a little shade to the north side of the old wooden building.

Agnes, somehow aware that she was being trampled on from above, scrabbled and scrambled as best she was able in the cramped space to get out of the hole. Putting her back fully to the task she heaved upwards with all her woollen might and propelled Father McIntosh and the set of steps a good half meter into the air.

"Jesus, Mary and Joseph!" yelled Father McIntosh as the steps fell on top of him. "It's a bloody earthquake," following which he was knocked briefly unconscious. He was just coming around and was rubbing his head when Belinda and Joe found him. "Did you feel that quake? Did you? Did you? Was the voice of God, that one!"

"I gotta feeling it was the sheep of God," said Joe to Belinda, spotting unmistakable signs of where the sheep had been as they helped Father McIntosh to his rather unsteady feet. They scanned the grounds for a sight of Agnes. She was not to be seen.

"Help me home, my children. I feel a mortal need for a drop of the hard stuff after that little to-do. The voice of God all right," said Father McIntosh.

"You shouldn't hit the hard stuff if you've got a concussion, Father," said Belinda. "My mum says . . ."

"Good woman that she is, does that mother of yours ever stop giving advice, young lady?" said Father McIntosh.

They rounded the corner of the church, Father McIntosh tottering slightly as Joe and Belinda assisted him. There in front of them, barring the way and with head lowered ready for another go, stood Agnes. "Ye Gods and little fishes!" cried Father McIntosh. "I reckon it's a Sasquatch!"

The sound of his powerful, preaching voice startled the sheep. In one bound Agnes found refuge in the middle of a large clump of blackberries. Almost as quickly as the priest had spotted her, she was gone.

"Don't think it was one of them, Father," said

Belinda. "That knock on your head has made you all groggy and seeing things."

"That's right Father," said Joe, "I think it was your cat. Yeah. It was your cat Mittens all right. All you saw was your cat Mittens," he repeated, very carefully.

"I can still tell a cat from a Sasquatch, boy. I tell you it was a Sasquatch! Groggy be damned. Only grog I want at this very moment is sitting in a bottle in the desk in my study. Now then, help me inside so I can get at it," said Father McIntosh.

It took a good twenty minutes to get Agnes out of the blackberry bush. The sheep was no help at all. As fast as Joe and Belinda untangled one bit of Agnes, she just as quickly wired herself securely into another tendril of the plant. Finally, she was free.

"This is no good," said the scratched and slightly bleeding Belinda rather unhappily as Agnes enthusiastically helped herself to a good square meal of bread and milk from Mrs. Wiggins's best Tupperware cake container. "What say we just hand her in to the cops and say we've found a lost sheep? We can't go on like this."

"They'll sure knock her on the head quick as look," said Joe. "Our cops are worse then Derek, Shane and Kevin all put together."

"Yeah, well, I guess you'd know about that better'n me," said Belinda. "I'm at my wits' end."

"You sure give up easy, eh?"

"You should talk," said Belinda. "It was you,

yesterday, who was all for letting Kevin have her."

"I got an idea," said Joe. "Where is the one place ever that no one would think of looking for Agnes?"

"Under your bed," said Belinda. "Come on. Let's try it."

Joe ignored her. "In a flock of sheep, of course," he announced.

"In a flock of sheep?"

"In a flock of sheep."

"Of course!" said Belinda.

"You know that paddock over the back of school?"

"Yep. It's part of old man Jones's farm. Of course I know it. So?"

"It's full of sheep," said Joe. "What we do is grab Agnes right now, or when it's nearly dark again — but not too long because Mum wants to know what I'm doing out so much at nights — and put her in with his sheep. No one'll ever know."

"I don't know . . ." Belinda shook her head.

"It'll work," said Joe, "I just know it'll work. All we have to do then is turn up once a day with her bread and milk. I reckon we can forget the cabbage for a while 'coz if you look at your feet you can see her bowels are working just great."

"Poo!" said Belinda looking down. "Stink!"

"Yep. Reckon they do," said Joe. "See, she'll mix in with all the others, make new friends and all that and who knows? Might not even want any bread and milk after a while and might just start to realize she is a sheep."

Belinda began to see more and more advantages. "You could be right," she said, "for a change. She might even get shorn and save us the worry of that. Who knows?" She extended her imagination even further. "She might find a mate and have some lambs."

"I hadn't thought of that," said Joe, looking at Agnes.

"Still," said Belinda, "I doubt it." She looked at the sheep and shook her head. "She's sure not the most attractive of sheep."

"Come on. Let's get a move on before Father McIntosh wakes up and wonders what we're still doing here."

This time it proved far easier to move Agnes from one place to another. She found fewer distractions along the way. Their only bad moment came when Joe thought he saw Bruce's pickup bearing down on them from the dusky distance. "They'll be out searching for her," he said. "I bet they will." Together they pushed the sheep into an open gateway and stood in front of her.

The pickup had cruised past — and it wasn't Kevin and Bruce — when a window in the house behind them opened and a man's voice called out, "You kids get your damn dog off my garden. Damn dogs fouling everywhere. Is nothing sacred these days?"

All of which hinted at the very major difficulties Mr. Jones's sheep were about to encounter when, for the first time in seven or eight years, Agnes came face to face with others of her own kind. Not that Joe and Belinda hung around long enough to find out. Shoving Agnes in through the gate of Mr. Jones's paddock, and making sure that the gate was well bolted behind her, they took off.

Agnes took the very closest of interest in the other sheep. She worked them from one end of the paddock to the other — several times! The other sheep protested so loudly that two nearby residents phoned Mr. Jones to complain. Fortunately for Agnes, Mr. Jones was out at the Rotary and Mrs. Jones told the callers there was nothing she could do and that her husband would investigate the next day.

Those of the sheep that protested most, got the treatment Agnes generally reserved only for the late Mrs. Carpenter's great-great-nephew, Shane Pike. Agnes spent most of a wonderful night getting to know her own kind again. By the next morning she had the creatures so brainwashed it was a relatively simple task to make them do exactly what she wanted. By the next morning what the other sheep wanted most was to get away from this strange, bullying creature that smelt a bit like them but acted more like a dog or, even worse, a human being. Driven by a strong urge to escape their tormentor, they found one small gap in Mr. Jones's fence. The force of their combined bodies made the small gap sufficiently large for them to escape from Agnes. Well, they almost escaped.

Mrs. Robinson had her whole class (other than the three or four who were hiding out in the loos) out on the school field for a quick, quieting-down workout, when Joe and Belinda next had their attention drawn to Agnes. "Hey! Look, you kids!" someone yelled. "Old Mr. Jones's sheep got in our field and there's a giant one driving them. Holy cow! Look at that giant sheep! It looks a bit like an elephant or a moose."

"Come on, you kids!" yelled another of Mrs. Robinson's pupils. "Let's get them back in old Jones's paddock."

"Stay where you are. All of you," said Mrs. Robinson, but she was too late. And then, "Come back here! This very instant!" There seemed even less point in calling out again so she took off after them.

Had Agnes been left to shepherd her flock as she saw fit, everything would have been all right. At least half all right. She might have taken them for one or two circuits of the school field. She might have herded them quietly around the town, with just an occasional nudge or two to the hindquarters of the slower and lazier members of her group if they needed any encouragement to get through the traffic. She might even, although this is less likely, have given up on the boring and stupid things altogether and made off alone to pastures fresh and new. However, none of this will ever be known. The sudden arrival of the whole of Mrs. Robinson's class — the loo-skulkers had quietly arrived because the sounds of a rodeo are quite, quite different from, and much more appealing than, the sounds of a quiet workout on the field — put a sudden stop to Agnes's quiet mid-morning amble.

The sight of Mrs. Robinson's class in full flight struck mild terror into the hearts of Mr. Jones's sheep and great joy into that of Agnes. The eyesight of an eight-year-old sheep is quite likely not so good as it originally was and the blurred sighting, much less the sound, of a whole horde of Shane-like creatures, was the next best thing to paradise.

"Come back here! Come back here!" Mrs. Robinson was in good voice. "Mary O'Donnell! Come here this instant and go get the principal."

No one listened. No one heard.

Seventeen of Mr. Jones's twenty-nine sheep ended up scrambling back home through the hole in his fence. Another six found similar holes in another fence and took refuge with three large bulls in a neighboring paddock. Four more got herded into the junior school flower garden and made mincemeat of several newly planted perennials, including a quite rare oriental poppy donated to them by Father McIntosh. The remaining two sheep were never seen again and all sorts of stories circulated about their gruesome fates for some weeks to come.

Agnes had the time of her life. She joined in

with one small group of runners that she thought were chasing another small group of runners. Six firm bunts of her head finished off the second group.

"Class! Class! Class!" Good teacher that she was, Mrs. Robinson never gave up. "Leave that thing alone. It's savage. It's berserk. I think it's got rabies!"

Agnes discovered another group of "Shanes" and helped them over the fence into the paddock of bulls. They didn't know which way to turn.

"You'll stay in after school, you mark my words!" Mrs. Robinson threatened. And then, more to herself than to her class who weren't listening anyway, "Why, in God's good name, didn't I take that checkout job at the Food Giant? This is sheer insanity."

"Don't you dare say anything," said Belinda to Joe as half-time approached.

"She's had it this time," said Joe.

"She has not," said Belinda. "Just watch where she goes and pretend to join in."

There was no need to pretend. Agnes had very quickly realized that her two closest friends were a part of this strange group and that really, all she was doing was getting rid of the strays so that she could once again have Joe and Belinda all to herself. This was certainly not going to be possible until she did something about a weird, arm-flapping and squealing shape that seemed to think it owned this paddock. The weird, arm-flapping creature was Mrs. Robinson.

The class actually tired of the sport and ran out of puff before the teacher. Mrs. Robinson was a well-known local jogger who had even once run a half-marathon. Eventually the field was reduced to just four — Belinda, Joe, Mrs. Robinson and Agnes. The others, very well worked-out by this stage, rested, spectators around the sidelines taking in the liveliest game the field had seen in many a long year.

"Line up! Line up! Line up!" Mrs. Robinson was getting hoarse.

"Get her in that corner!" yelled Joe. "Bale her up! Bale her up!"

"We can't bale up Mrs. Robinson," Belinda called back to him, "it wouldn't be nice."

"Not her!" yelled Joe. "Agnes!"

"Agnes? Who's Agnes?" yelled Mrs. Robinson.

"Baaaaaaa!" yelled Agnes coming in to circle Mrs. Robinson like a woollen vulture.

"Hell's bells, it's me bloody sheep!" yelled Kevin, who was biking down the road with a parcel of meat he was delivering to a senior citizen who had the flu. He dumped his bike and the meat and jumped the fence, not noticing the large German shepherd dog that had been tossing up whether or not to join Mrs. Robinson, Joe, Belinda, Agnes and all the fun. At the last moment it decided to join Kevin's parcel instead.

Kevin never really got into the game at all, which was a pity. After all, he knew this field well. It had been the scene of many of his rugby triumphs. On this occasion he arrived just in time to carry Mrs. Robinson back to the principal's office, followed by all of Mrs. Robinson's class except for Belinda and Joe who were last spotted heading for the pine plantation in hot pursuit of Agnes the sheep.

There were some of Mrs. Robinson's class who swore that Agnes had catapulted their teacher at least as high as one of the rugby goalposts, if not higher. The only one in her class who was good at math tried to explain that it was all a matter of momentum and physics but no one else listened. More than a few said that they heard quite clearly — and it was a bit like a .22 rifle shot — the crack of Mrs. Robinson's ankle breaking as she landed back on the field from which Agnes had removed her only seconds earlier.

8

Agnes Finds a Haven

In a country of over fifty million sheep and only three million people it is surprising that the former don't make the human interest newspaper stories more often than they do. Agnes's great athletic feat with Mrs. Robinson went virtually unreported in the local press. **Wild Sheep Attacks Elderly Woman** ran the headline and there was very little more information in the short paragraph that followed. Mrs. Robinson considered writing a letter to the editor pointing out one fundamental error in the brief report. However, as she rested at home she reflected that it was certainly half right and, really, she had never felt more elderly in all her life.

By the time Kevin had got back out on the field after helping the principal, the ambulance driver and a few of Mrs. Robinson's class tuck Mrs. Robinson as comfortably as possible into the ambulance, not only was Agnes well gone but so was the parcel of meat for the senior citizen, and so was his bike. The bike had been borrowed by one of Mrs. Robinson's students for a quick trip into town and then home for lunch. The German shepherd had also gone. Kevin felt murderous. "Least it's still alive . . ." he muttered as he started walking, "till I get my hands on it."

"I think our Joe's got his first girlfriend," said Mrs. Walsh to her husband. "We don't see hide nor hair of him these days, do we dear? And do you know what?" She did not wait for a reply. "Old Granny Smith down the road tells me she's even seen them out walking together in the evenings with a big Great Dane."

"Wonder where he nicked the dog from?" said Joe's brother, Eddie.

"Have not got a girlfriend," said Joe, blushing a bright scarlet.

"Nothing wrong with having a girlfriend, boy," said his father. "Why, I even had one once. Pity I hadn't kept it that way," he said, winking at them.

"Well she must be blind," said Eddie. "Joe's one, I mean, Dad. Not your old one."

"Probably why she walks round with him in the evenings," said Mr. Walsh.

"Yeah," said Eddie, "and the Great Dane's a seeing-eye dog." Joe's elder brother and father spent the next few minutes chuckling and winking and punching at Joe until Mrs. Walsh shut them both up by sharply ordering them to do the dishes. Having got the two of them out of the way she patted the seat beside her for Joe to sit down.

"Who is she, dear?" she asked him sweetly. "You can tell your old mum."

"Tell my old mum what?" asked Joe.

"Oh, my baby's blushing again and what a blush it is with that mop of red hair and all those freckles." Mrs. Walsh put an arm around her younger son. "Ah, me. Young love. I guess it had to attack even you sometime or other," she smiled, "and it's most certainly doing wonders for your appetite. I counted up and it was thirteen loaves of bread we got through last week."

"It wasn't Mrs. Robinson's fault, Mum. I don't think she wanted to break her ankle. It's no good writing to the principal again. Father McIntosh is only teaching us till she can walk on crutches," said Belinda. "And it's not his fault either."

"That's as may be, Belinda. But what, may I ask if I may be permitted, was that woman doing out on the field chasing sheep in the first place, when she should have been inside? That's what we pay her for, teaching her class."

"Seems much the same sort of job to me," said Mr. Wiggins reasonably. "More chance knocking a bit of sense into a flock of sheep than those kids at that school these days. Sure gone down the drain since the days you'n me went there, Vi."

"I fully intend dropping a line to the Bishop,"

said Mrs. Wiggins. "Of all people he should know what's going on down there and I know you're seeing that dreadful Joe Walsh boy, Belinda, and if his mother smirks at me once more when I'm in the Food Giant I don't know what I'll do and we forever seem to be bumping into each other at the bread stands these days. I forget who it was said to me they saw you and him out together one evening last week riding a Shetland pony and how on earth that Walsh family can afford ponies and they owe money all over town and he's probably on the dole I'll bet my last dollar I'll never know. Keep away from him, Belinda. I mean that."

"Yes, Mum," said Belinda.

"Pass me my writing pad dear and make us a cup of tea, there's an angel."

It was bliss and it was heaven and at last they found a haven for Agnes. It was well up into the pine plantation and just off the road. The only other living creatures within sight or earshot were a large and loud family of magpies, a couple of rabbits and Mrs. Carmen Sylvester. Agnes showed no great interest in any of them. Truth to tell, Agnes appeared to appreciate the isolation and the peace and quiet after the events and excitement of the last few days.

Getting her to her new home unobserved had proved to be next to no hassle. Belinda and Joe found themselves enjoying the peace and quiet as much as the sheep.

There had been only the one house to pass. That of Mrs. Carmen Sylvester, Chairperson of the Drama Society, who had lived alone since Mr. Sylvester had decided some years before that enough was enough and, if "all the world is a stage" as his wife often told him, he'd be much happier on some other part of it.

"My mum says she's a weirdo," whispered Belinda as they edged Agnes past the Sylvester cottage. "She's written to the authorities about her. My mum says she should be in an institution."

"Your mum should?" asked Joe.

"There she is," Belinda whispered again and pointed. "What d'you reckon she's doing?"

Mrs. Carmen Sylvester, fully absorbed in her work, did not notice Belinda, Joe, or Agnes. She was kneeling in the shade of a fully grown gingko tree, on an old bit of carpet. With every ounce of her concentration she appeared to be peeling the carpet with a knife as if it were a potato or a carrot. "I better tell Mum she's getting worse," said Belinda. "She'll need to know for her next letter."

"Baaa," said Agnes, rather tiredly.

"I thought I'd just see if she'd come back, Mr. Pike," Kevin said to Derek.

Kevin caught Derek by surprise and for one shocking moment the man thought the boy was referring to the late Mrs. Carpenter. "Who? Who's come back?"

"That old sheep," said Kevin. "You seen her again?"

"It's not really good enough young man," said Moira, joining her husband. "She's an old, old animal and not to be blamed and my husband, Mr. Pike that is, trusted you to give her a kind and peaceful end. Now you've mislaid her. I just hope the SPCA don't get onto this and blame us in any way. She deserved better and it's not our fault at all."

"Yeah," said Shane.

"Just thought she might come back here," said Kevin.

"She's not a homing pigeon," said Derek sharply.

"Nah, she's not no homing pigeon," said Shane. "She should be a dead duck, eh? Except you stuffed it up. Tell me when you get her, Kevin. You promised."

"That's not nice, Shaney dear," said Moira.

"Haven't got all day to stand round yakking," said Derek, "unless you want to give a hand. The movers are here tomorrow. The old place is on the move and it's got to be jacked up first."

"Sorry, Mr. Pike," said Kevin, "gotta go to the cops — police, I mean. They think they found me bike and I still got some meat I gotta deliver." He turned and made his way out of what was left of the late Mrs. Carpenter's garden of knocked-down and well-mashed camellias, rhododendrons, and magnolias.

"And you find that old sheep, young man,"

Moira called after him. "I simply do not like the idea of her all lost and upset and in the traffic or whatever."

"I do," said Shane. "She could get squashed by one of them sheep trucks," he giggled. "That'd be cool."

"Such a nice polite boy, that," said Moira to Derek and Shane as Kevin clambered into his mate Bruce's pickup and made room for himself beside their two young pig dogs, Spot and Woofer. "It's just a pity there aren't more like him." She looked at her Shane. "Someone was telling me just the other day that his mum's been nominated for Mother of the Year and will probabaly win it too. That would certainly make her arthritis more worthwhile. She's devoted to him, of course, and that doesn't surprise me. Any mother would be. That beautiful head of hair!" said Moira but Derek was no longer listening to her. Back bent, he was under the house again, jacking and bracing and readying the old building for its removal. Shane was not listening either. Sheep may well not be homing pigeons but you never could tell with one like Agnes. Shane scouted the battered under-growth of his late great-great-aunt's garden plus those of the next three houses down, just in case. Better to be sure than sorry.

No Agnes.

Over the next few days Belinda and Joe gathered as many odds and ends of old sawed timber that they could find. "Why can't you just nick what we need from the timber yard?" Belinda said to Joe. "It'd be easier and it's much nearer. My dad was saving this stuff to box his lettuces and I know he'll miss it and I sure don't want to be round when he finds it's gone. I got us some bits from old Mrs. Carpenter's. I think that Derek is pulling her house down. It's dreadful."

During the hour or so of dusk over these few days they hauled the timber piece by piece up into the hills. "Tried to get old Jacko's new bike," said Joe, "only his old man said he wasn't allowed to let it out of his sight, not ever. Bikes get pinched just so easy these days. We could've tied all this on and done it all in no time."

"Jacko hasn't got a bike," said Belinda. "They can't afford one for him."

"He's got one now. He got it last week," said Joe. "He got it on that day Mrs. Robinson broke her ankle. It was second-hand and his old man spray-painted it for him."

The two of them built a very rough-and-ready shelter for Agnes making use of three pine trees that had the misfortune to be growing too close together, plus assorted bits and pieces of wood and a sheet of corrugated iron that had blown off the porch roof at St. Joseph's Church and which Father McIntosh had not got round to nailing up again. Securely dog-chained to one of the trees, and with a thick mattress of dry pine needles beneath her and the security of wood and iron around and above her, Agnes could now begin a contented and peaceful retirement, looking forward to a once-daily feed of bread and milk.

Belinda and Joe breathed easier. Leaning back on another bed of pine needles Joe said, "I just hope old Mrs. Carpenter is up there looking down and is fully grateful for all we've done for her sheep."

"She won't be," said Belinda firmly.

"She said she would be," said Joe. "I bet she is. She'll be grateful all right."

"Well she won't be," repeated Belinda. "I checked with my mum."

"So, your mum's God now, is she?" said Joe, slightly nastily.

"She knows," said Belinda.

"Yeah. She thinks she knows everything, your mum. Bet she doesn't know where all those bits of wood are." He nodded at their sheep house.

"Look," said Belinda, determined not to get upset at what Joe said about her mother, "old Mrs. Carpenter, at the very, very best, will be in limbo. Limbo's the sort of halfway place. She was a Presbyterian and they don't go straight to heaven; not like us. They're not allowed to. Father McIntosh said not even the ones who are very good. Somehow or other out in limbo they get sorted out. Some do get sent on to heaven after a few tests and a bit of a wait."

"I guess your mum knows. Did she write to the Pope about it, eh?" Joe asked slyly.

"But wherever she is," Belinda said, ignoring him, "I'm sure she'll be feeling very grateful. I know I would be if I was her and we sure have done our best with old Agnes. Now come on, we can't hang around here forever. It's changing my whole life as it is and not very much for the better either. Agnes is making me lose all my old friends."

"That's one good thing she's done then," said Joe. "I'd sure as hell rather have Agnes the sheep than your friends any day. Come on." He looked up through the trees. "It's gonna rain."

9
Nothing About Agnes

Except for the letter Belinda's mother, Mrs. Wiggins, wrote to Joe's mother, Mrs. Walsh, everything was peaceful and quiet for some time. People don't have very long memories and those around who had some vague remembrance of a large, bad-tempered and heavily coated sheep soon forgot them.

Other things were happening. Mrs. Robinson hobbled back to school and to Room Five. She found the experience of being on crutches did have its teaching advantages and rewards. While far too kindly and nice a person to deliberately throw a crutch, or whack or maim someone with a crutch, or even poke them with a crutch, it was still amazing how wonderfully well you could slow things down with such things as a crutch carelessly left lying across a doorway or aisle of desks. Father McIntosh, for one, was delighted to welcome her back. "You're welcome to the little monsters, girl," he said.

"Father!" Mrs. Robinson was quite shocked. "It's only little children you're talking about!"

"Children! *Children!* You call them children? Beasts, that's what they are. Every one of them. Little tykes!"

Most evenings Kevin would wander out and about in the town. "Got to exercise Spot, Mum," he would say, patting his half of his and Bruce's pig dog team.

"You just put a scarf on, dearie. And a woolly hat, there's a good boy," said his mother. "There's still a nip in the air and it's more than a bit clammy and you know it goes straight to your chest and a hacking cough every time."

"Aw, Mum. Nuthin' wrong with me chest," said Kevin, and there wasn't much wrong with it either. After all, he was now in his second season playing fly-half for the third division Rovers rugby team and had never had a game off for a hacking cough or cold in all that time. Most certainly there were more than a few of the younger, female fans of rugby on the sideline who would dearly have loved to get to know his particular chest.

"And while I know and admit that our boys in blue, our police, do a wonderful job for our community dear, it is a surprise to me that they haven't done more to find your bicycle. When I think of all those newspapers you delivered for so many years in the icy cold just to pay for it . . ." continued his mother.

"Aw, Mum," he said. "Come Christmas I'll have enough to put away for me pickup, eh?"

"Just so long as it isn't a motorbike, darling," said Myra. "The toll that the motorcycle has taken on our youth and young people of today is a national disaster and tragedy . . . but I know I can trust you, of course. My boy!" And she would give him a hug and wave to him from behind the net curtains of the lounge window as he walked off down the driveway between the two straight lines of standard roses he had recently helped her to prune. What a lovely boy! And then she would sit down again to work on her speech for the Mother of the Year contest.

Kevin would exercise Spot. Together they would check the town's two car yards for any new pickups that might have been traded in since the previous day. Then they would take a different street each night and carefully reconnoiter all properties in order to see if Agnes had perhaps found a new home. Finally, Kevin and Spot would call on Kevin's best mate, Bruce, and his half of the pig dog team, Woofer, who were dead lucky enough to have their own small, detached room with its own toilet, right down at the bottom of Bruce's parents' garden and well away from the main house. Kevin and Bruce would spend a happy hour looking through the same pig and deer hunting books they had looked through the night before, drinking one

or two bottles of beer, smoking a couple of ciga-
rettes each and using bad language.

Kevin and Bruce had known each other for so
long that very few words were necessary in their
conversations. "D'ya seat, mate?" one would say,
pointing to a picture of a stuck and bleeding pig
and inviting the attention of the other.

"Bewd-ay, mate?" A sort of approval.

"G-yerg." A sort of drinking sound. "G-yerg, g-
yerg, g-yerg . . ."

"Top yup, mate?" Invitation to more beer.

"Cha-ketcha-druck?" A friendly inquiry about
getting Bruce's vehicle from the garage where the
fitting of bull-bars to the front was being done
rather slowly. The bull-bars were necessary for upcoming pig hunts.

"Cha-fine-ya-sodden sheep, mate?" Inquiry
about a wet sheep? About Agnes?

"Nah."

"Top yup?" The favorite expression and the one
used most often.

"Grade A, mate," which might have been a comment on the rugby team they hoped one day to
be asked to play for. Or it could have been, "Gray
day, mate," a comment on the type of weather
that was particularly frequent in these parts.

And so it would go on until, having fully covered
all events of interest that had taken place since the
day before and having fully exhausted all conver-
sational possibilities, Kevin would take off, chew-
ing a fistful of peppermints and already looking

forward to the mug of hot Horlicks his mum would have ready for him.

About now, Derek and Moira spent most evenings doing bills. This became more necessary on the day the jacking up of the late Mrs. Carpenter's house went a centimeter or so too far and the old building gently, very slowly and very definitely, gave up the ghost. It split in two and slid from its temporary foundation to rest in two pieces back on the earth from which Derek had hoisted it.

Derek found out that the moving firm didn't insure the jacking-up if you insisted on doing it yourself to save money. "How unfair and unjust," said Moira. "I think you should sue them, dear. Go down and see Mr. Claude Cotter tomorrow morning. Go on!" she ordered. "You must."

Mr. Cotter was of no help and no comfort; also pointing out that the late Mrs. Carpenter had carried no insurance coverage whatsoever for many years on any of her property at all. On the whole, she had considered the insurance industry an exercise in daylight robbery conducted by a pack of sharks.

Nothing that he, Mr. Cotter, could tell her had changed her mind. Not that it mattered anyway and certainly any insurance that the old lady might have carried would not have covered the raising of a ninety-year-old building two meters into the air.

"I told her, lad. Many a time I told her," said

Mr. Cotter shaking his head. "But you know what the old girl was like. Good Lord, boy, I shuddered some nights thinking of that priceless collection of antique floor rugs the old girl owned. Priceless, all of them. Would've given my eye teeth — false and all as they are — for just one of those old rugs."

"Erg — ug — ruh — rug?"

"What's that, lad? Speak up! The old hearing, you know."

"Erg — rug . . . ?"

"You can rest assured lad, that the very first thing I did when she gifted — all legal and above board — that load of Chinese blue and white porcelain to those two kiddies who looked after her pet lamb, was safe-deposit and insure the stuff. Dear old lady, it was only a couple of months before she died."

"Chuh — chuh — chuh — Chinese?" said Derek, with a slight choking sound.

Mr. Claude Cotter chuckled at him. "Eccentric old bird. King's ransom it's worth, chipped and all. Two lucky kiddies, those two. My word they are. Not that they know it. Not yet. She thought the world of them."

"Chuh — chuh — chuh . . . all legal?"

"Of course, lad. That's what she wanted. Cost her a tidy pile in valuations and gift duties, not to mention my fees. Still, that's what she wanted. She insisted. Mind you, most of that would have come out of what you're to get." Mr. Cotter chuckled at the thought. "Wonderful old lady. Wonderful!"

"Wonderful," said Derek, clenching one fist and softly pounding it into the opened palm of his other hand.

Dear Mrs. Walsh,

It would please my husband and I if you would kindly order your son Joe, the one who is altar boy at St. Joseph's on the last Sunday in every month if you don't know which one I mean, to keep away from our young daughter Belinda. Belinda has had a sheltered and good upbringing which I cannot expect you to know and understand but is quite true and it is come to my attention and she is allergic.

My husband and I are concerned parents and I am telling the school and speak as I find, which is best. Do as I would be done is my motto in life and I'm sure you done your best with your boy, but he is not to be and my husband and I agree.

Yours faithfully,
Mrs. Wiggins
E & O E

"Who is E and O E?" asked Mr. Walsh.

"Search me. Ask her husband. It's probably him," said Mrs. Walsh. "Do as she should be done by? I'll happily do Vi Wiggins any day of the flaming week!"

"Should hear what they say down the club about

both of them," said her husband. "Him and her."

"What am I going to do? What am I going to do?" Mrs. Walsh's voice rose. "What am I going to do?" A louder wail. "You can deal with it. He's your son too!"

"Do you have to keep on reminding me?" Mr. Walsh sounded tired. "Joe!" he called. "Joe! Get the hell in here!"

Joe came through into the kitchen from the bedroom he shared with Eddie and in which he had just spent a useless and fruitless half hour working on finding the combination of Eddie's boom box/headboard padlock. "Whaddya want?" he asked nicely.

"Keep away from that damned girl or I'll thrash you within an inch of your rotten little life and put you through the wringer. Geddit?"

"What's up, Mum?" asked Joe.

"You will not lay a fist on that child," said Mrs. Walsh to her husband. "Over my dead body. How dare you!"

"You asked me to deal with it," said Mr. Walsh reasonably. "It's always the same. The minute I start to straighten them out . . ."

"Her precious daughter indeed," said Mrs. Walsh. "I've seen her. Oh yes, I've seen her all right."

"Seen who?" asked Joe.

"Just you keep away from her dear," said his mother.

"Who?" asked Joe, and sensing his mother's

softness towards him, "Can I have a cookie?"

"Allergic indeed!" said Mrs. Walsh.

"What's allergic?" asked Joe. "Can I have a cookie?"

"The cheek! The cheek of that woman . . ."

"Yeah, I know," said Joe. "Who?"

"Violet Whatshername. Oh, yes! I could tell you a thing or two about her when we were all at school. No better than she should be. None of that family were!"

"Who?" asked Joe. "Cookie, Mum? Please?"

"Come here," she said to Joe. He obeyed her and she gave him a big hug. "My boy," she said.

"Please can I have a cookie, Mum? One of those chocolate ones in the tin at the back?"

"Tin at the back?" His mother's voice lost all its softness. "I was saving those for when Grandma Walsh came. You know how she loves them. You haven't . . . ?" She got up from her chair and walked to the cupboard, opened it, checked her tins. "You have! You little monster!"

"Can I belt him now? Please?" begged Mr. Walsh, a gleam of anticipation in his eye.

But Joe had gone.

10
Agnes Meets a New Friend and Encounters an Old Enemy

The sight of Mrs. Carmen Sylvester at her spinning wheel, singing softly to herself and to Agnes who lay stretched out asleep at her feet, struck a mixture of feelings into Joe and Belinda.

She's dead, thought Joe, as he eyed the still form of Agnes. He whispered, "Thank you our Father in Heaven for letting Mrs. Sylvester finish her off."

Mum's right, thought Belinda, as she eyed Mrs. Carmen Sylvester. She's mad! She should be in an institution. She whispered to Joe, "What do we do now?"

"Go home," whispered Joe.

Too late. "Aha, my two little sheep-keepers. A shepherd and a shepherdess but not, alas, of Dresden." Then she sang to them. " 'Nymphs and Shepherds come away, come away . . .' "

"Wha — ?" said Joe.

" 'Come out, come out from your sylvan glade,

and games that nymphs have oft-times played
. . .' " Mrs. Sylvester beckoned.

"Baaaa . . ." said Agnes, waking up.

"Arise, dear lamb! Get up on your feet! Bleat
bleat bleat, bleat bleat, bleat bleat!" she finished
somewhat unusually, before breaking into another
song about sheep safely grazing in a paddock.

"What you doing with our sheep?" asked Joe.

"You leave her alone," said Belinda.

"You're stealing all her wool," said Joe.

"Well, she's got enough of it," said Mrs. Sylvester reasonably. "Take me more than a month of
Sundays to munch my way through this little pile
of fluff." She patted Agnes. The sheep, unusually,
seemed to quite enjoy the attention from this
stranger.

"You're still stealing it," said Joe.

"Well, she's on public property," said Mrs.
Sylvester. "Besides, she gave me permission." She
patted Agnes again. "Didn't you, my little ovine
friend?" Then followed another snatch of song
about flocks in pastures green abiding.

"Baaaa," said Agnes in a sort of chorus, and
Mrs. Sylvester bent over the animal and snipped
off a couple more thickish hanks of dirty and greasy
wool.

"Ah, my children," she said to Belinda and Joe,
"my heart's desire has always been to spin from
the sheep's back, to lather the strands in the trick-
ling force of a clear mountain stream and to dye

93

the silken, well, woollen thread in a potent brew of natural moss and lichens."

"Eh?" said Belinda.

"Look, kids," said Mrs. Sylvester. "Saw you two, together or alone, climb my rocky path into these pine trees. Aha, thought Carmen, what hanky-panky's going on up there day after day? Up I trek. What do I find? One old sheep with more wool than she knows what to do with and anxious for a bit of company. What gives, kids?" she demanded of Joe and Belinda.

"Eh?" said Joe.

"Spill the beans," said Mrs. Sylvester.

"Eh?" said Belinda.

"I fear this tangled tale is going to take us a long time in the telling," said Mrs. Sylvester. "A very long while indeed."

When the story was done she then said, "Oh, what a tale you have spun, spun, spun. And from the wicked butcher you have run, run, run," and she patted Agnes.

"No. Kevin's not really wicked. He's really quite nice and he can't help his job or his bloody nature," said Belinda.

"And he is a credit and a great blessing to his mother," said Joe who had now heard this quite often.

"So are you, dear boy. So are you. Has no one ever told you that?"

"Not often," lied Joe.

"Never." Belinda told the truth.

"Such an inspiration! Such devotion to an old animal. My heart is touched," said Mrs. Sylvester.

"And that's not all," said Joe under his breath. "But I still don't think you should just nick her wool without asking," he said aloud. "You won't tell anyone she's here?" he asked anxiously.

"My lips are sealed," said Mrs. Sylvester and she sang a bit more about nymphs and shepherds. "It shall be our little secret. Look kids, I'd take her down to Yew Tree Cottage — my little pad — and give her a good home if I thought it would help, but as it is I've hardly got enough room to swing a cat, much less an overgrown sheep. Besides, I can just tell that Agnes would play merry hell with my three new daphne bushes. My word, was I lucky to get them. It's that sweet-scented one you know."

Belinda was direct. "Okay. You can spin bits of her wool if she'll let you and you can bring her stuff to eat in exchange. Him and me," she pointed to Joe, "we'll make you a list. Fair's fair!"

"Quid pro quo," said Mrs. Carmen Sylvester.

"Eh?" Belinda and Joe said together.

"It's the cabbage that gives us the most trouble," said Belinda.

"I know the feeling, darling," said Mrs. Sylvester. "Can be sheer agony for those of us over forty."

"Twice a week she needs it. Just lightly boiled. It's for her bowels and regularity," said Belinda.

"Yeah," said Joe, "It's to make her . . ."

"I know exactly what she means, dear boy," said Mrs. Sylvester quickly.

"And if you get any old or spare bread it would be a help," said Belinda. "It's getting very hard for us and my mum's taking me to the doctor next week to get checked for something called carbo-hydrate dependency."

"I shall do my level best, darlings, and I shall fill a thermos, my angels of mercy, and whenever my busy schedule permits I shall join you herein this fairy grotto for a goblet of nectar and a libation to the gods."

"Shoot!" said Joe. "Sounds great. What is it? Is it booze?"

"No, darling. It'll be a cup of tea." Mrs. Sylvester sang another verse about the nymphs and the shepherds after which she picked up her spinning wheel and trudged off down the hill and back to Yew Tree Cottage.

"I dunno," said Belinda. "Can we trust her? She sure is a loony."

"I dunno either," said Joe. "Still, she's not much more strange than old Mrs. Carpenter, or Mrs. Robinson. She's not much more strange than your mum, come to think of it . . ."

Some things are too good to be true. Belinda's and Joe's arrangement with Mrs. Carmen Sylvester in regard to catering for Agnes up in her pine tree retirement home was one of them. It was Shane

Pike and his friend Crispin who messed things up.

Willing to do almost anything to get away from home and the increasingly bad-tempered Derek and yet another Saturday searching the dump for Mrs. Carpenter's old carpets, Shane sneaked out of the Pike house and met up with Crispin. Together they stole the air rifle belonging to Crispin's older brother. It was under the brother's bed and they had much difficulty getting it out from its hiding place and out of the house without waking up the brother.

It was very early. Shoved down Crispin's jacket and jeans, the air rifle did make walking difficult. "Geez, Crispy. Looks like you got a wooden leg, eh?" said Shane. "Hurry up!"

"I can't," said Crispin.

They headed for a hunting trip up into the pine plantation, passing on the way Mrs. Carmen Sylvester's Yew Tree Cottage. "Wowee! Geez, she's sure gotta lot of carpets, eh?" said Crispin as they paused to peer over her gate and saw her clothesline and the lower branches of the gingko tree all festooned with slowly drying rugs.

"Just wish we had some more of them," said Shane, miserably. "Come on, Crispy. We're not even in the trees yet and I got me an urge to kill something, real bad."

"Me too," said Crispin, limping after his friend. "What can we kill?"

"Anything," said Shane. "There's magpies and birds and I even seen a rabbit once."

They hunted.

Shane took shots at two magpies, a half dozen sparrows, a blackbird, a tree trunk and a beer can. He missed them all. Crispin took aim and fired at the same two magpies, five different sparrows, the tree trunk and the beer can and Mr. Jones's Jersey bull over the fence in a paddock next to the pine plantation. He missed them all, too, although there was some argument that he might have scored a hit on the fence post that stood between him and the bull.

The hunt did not really get off the ground, so to speak, until they discovered the tethered Agnes. All of a sudden they were able to promote their hunt from small game (except, perhaps, for the bull) to big game. Well, bigger game.

"Who'd tie an old wild sheep in the middle of a forest, eh?" said Crispin, who spotted Agnes first. "Mad!"

"*Yerkurch cheep?!*" said Shane, pulling himself up the slippery pine-needled slope behind his friend, then peering out from a vantage point of safety directly behind Crispin's shoulder at the tied-up Agnes. "It's her," he breathed, puffing and panting. "It's her! It's her! It's that bloody old cow."

"It's not a cow, Shaney," said Crispin in disbelief. "You gettin' blind? It's a sheep."

"I know what it is." Shane edged behind a pine tree. "Giz the gun!" He stuck out a hand. "Giz the gun!" Just the smooth, hard feel of the weapon made him feel a lot, lot safer and more secure as he continued to peer between the pine needles and into the face of his longtime enemy. His pulse raced and a fever of excitement sweated its way onto his forehead. He wiped his eyes. His pulse and fever quickened even further as he saw Agnes was well and truly securely chained.

"Baaaaa," said Agnes, suddenly aware of the presence of an old playmate. "Baaaaa," and she rattled her chains and her dags.

"Nice sheep," said Crispin moving forward, hand outstretched.

"Keep away from it!" cried Shane. "It's just about the most dangerous, vicious sheep in the world and I should know. It belongs to my dad."

"Why's he tied it up here?" asked Crispin reasonably. "It's a long way from your house."

"It's a stolen sheep. Poachers took it, or sheep stealers."

"Why?" Crispin looked at Agnes, seeing no visible reason why anyone would want to steal this decrepit animal. "Oh, it's a stud, eh?" he said knowingly. "Like one of those valuable ones you breed from. Is it a prize ram?" Crispin knelt down and looked under Agnes to check. "Geez, it's sure gotta lotta wool. Can't see nuthin' at all."

"I'm gonna shoot it," said Shane.

"Okay," said Crispin. "You sure it's your old man's? You could be in trouble."

"Right between the eyes," said Shane.

"Well, you better get closer," said Crispin. "I don't reckon that gun'll shoot anything unless you get real, real close. Like right up to it and touching it."

Shane's pulse, breathing and fever almost reached exploding point. He loaded the air rifle and edged slowly out from the protection of the pine tree. He moved ever so carefully and gently around behind Crispin and into the sylvan glade that was the home and territory of his mortal enemy, Agnes. Agnes stood still. She eyed her old friend as he, eyes squinting against a shaft of sunlight, gingerly, delicately and oh-so-slowly, extended the rifle and pointed it towards her head.

Was this some succulent twig to be eaten? may have been the thought crossing Agnes's mind. What new little tidbit was this being proffered?

In his great and all-consuming brainstorm, Shane had not noticed the full extent of Agnes's tethering and the rather long coil of chain that lay on the ground behind her. Warning bells did not begin to ring in his tortured mind until far, far too late.

Slowly . . . slowly . . . one step further. Another. Too late! Too far! Too late! As Shane's finger curved nervously, trembling, on the trigger of the rifle, Agnes joined the action.

She got him this time full force just below the knees with the crown of her head. Shane's knees buckled as Agnes's neck lifted and jackknifed explosively. Had the boys on the forestry work program not recently practiced their silviculture pruning techniques in this small plantation of *pinus radiata*, Shane would have been prevented from flying very high by low-growing branches and would likely have fallen to earth, deposited at Agnes's feet, ready for her to have another go. As it was, he flew nonstop, directly upwards towards the sky. As he reached the apex of his flight he shot out his arms and grabbed. This was how he ended up clinging to the pine tree trunk like a koala, directly above Agnes and several meters from the ground.

Agnes gave the tree trunk a playful bunt or two but as yet the fruit was not ripe enough to fall.

Meanwhile, the air rifle had travelled a slightly different course over Shane's shoulder to connect quite brutally with Crispin's skull before slipping away, unnoticed, into a giant drift of pine needles. Crispin slithered the extent of the slope, howling rather loudly, before picking himself up to reverse-slither back up towards his friend and towards Agnes. "Where are ya, Shaney?"

"Up here," a small voice called.

"Where?" Crispin searched the ground.

"Here!"

"Can't see ya." Crispin continued the ground search.

"Look up!"

"Watcha doin' up there? Get down."

"Can't. I can't . . ." Shane started to shiver and clung harder to the tree trunk. "She'll kill me."

"Yeah. She might, I think. Yeah, I think she would," said Crispin seriously. Then he brightened up. "Still, fair enough, eh? You were tryin' to kill her. How long you gonna stay up there? I gotta go home now. Where's me gun? See ya at school Monday."

The fevered excitement had cooled on Shane's forehead. It changed to fevered terror at the thought of being deserted by his mate. "Hey, don't go! Don't leave me! Please, Crispy, don't leave me!"

"Got to, Shaney," said Crispin reasonably. "You know what my old lady's like if I'm late for lunch. You'll get down sometime. I think. Where's the gun?" Crispin had not known what struck his skull.

Cunning beat terror. "I got it up here with me, Crispy. You gotta do as I say, Crispy, else you'll never see it again. Not never — and I'll tell your father." As clearly and as carefully as he could from his koalalike position on the tree, Shane gave Crispin his orders. These involved running at great speed to the butcher's shop. They also involved Kevin, Kevin's butchering knife, Bruce's pickup and, finally, very large and very satisfying streams of gushing blood on a bed of pine needles.

11
Agnes Leaves
the Sylvan Glade

Joe, carrying two loaves of stale bread, and Belinda, carrying a carton of milk and a jam jar of sugar, met Crispin at the corner of the road just short of Mrs. Carmen Sylvester's Yew Tree Cottage. The lady herself was busy moving her collection of oriental rugs into her shed out of the way of direct sunlight, in which a fading of their natural dyes was possible. She was also thinking of selecting a winter cabbage from her vegetable garden when she heard voices on the roadway near her home.

"What's the hurry?" Belinda called out to Crispin as he rushed past.

"Is your bum on fire?" called Joe.

Crispin stopped and turned to face them, breathless. "There's this savage sheep up in them trees." Puff . . . puff . . . puff. "It's attacked me mate — he's Shaney Pike — up a tree. Gonna shoot him."

"Shoot Shane Pike?" asked Joe delightedly. "Good idea."

"Nah." Puff . . . puff . . . puff. "Shoota sheep." Puff . . . puff. He breathed heavily for a moment or two. "Gotta get help and get me gun back and Kevin at the butcher's." More heavy breathing. "Then it's gonna get killed good, eh?" The young hunter staggered off down the road puffing and muttering, "Me gun, me gun, me gun back. Gotta get me gun back."

"Shoot!" said Belinda, and then, "Shoot?" and she broke into a run just as Mrs. Carmen Sylvester, having recognized two of the voices, came through the gate.

"Here!" Mrs. Sylvester thrust a cabbage into Joe's hands. "I thought it must be my noble shepherd and shepherdess. She can have it raw today, slugs and all. I'm sick of the stink of cooked cabbage throughout the house. Raw cabbage is just as good for regularity. I tried it myself."

"They've got Agnes!" Joe cried, passing the cabbage back to her like a rugby football travelling out to the wing. "She's in great and deadly danger."

"Bless my soul," said Mrs. Sylvester, "so that's what it was all about." She tossed the cabbage over the fence and joined Joe and Belinda in the race up the hill into the pine plantation.

Belinda won. She had enjoyed a good headstart over the others and had missed out on playing with the cabbage. Joe was second. Mrs. Carmen Sylvester was a poor third. By the time the second and third runners arrived, Belinda had armed herself with a long, straight branch — one of those left by the trainee silviculturalists — and, with Agnes's help, was doing her post to poke the poor "koala" off the tree.

"You despicable little wretched worm!" Belinda was so furious she was using words she had never used before and had only previously heard coming from the mouth of her mother. Prod, prod, prod. Agnes had her forelegs up the tree trunk and was gazing fondly upwards and panting, tongue lolling out. "You cowardly little punk!" yelled Belinda. "I'll teach you a lesson you'll be a long time forgetting!" as she poked Shane on a soft part of his anatomy. "Get down! Get down this very instant!"

"Leave him there! Leave him there!" yelled Joe, clambering up the last of the slippery slope.

"No way!" cried Belinda, doing some more poking. "I'm going to stuff this slimey little creep in Agnes's house and I'm going to tie him up in there and it's going to be a lot of fun. Just let me poke him a few more times first." She managed to climb a step or two up the tree trunk in order to poke more satisfactorily.

All this time, Shane was yelping out quite pitifully. "Help-help-help-me, no-no-no-no don't do that, it hurts, help-help," knowing, deep within him, that his choices were limited. Did he let go and fall into the hands of this ferocious girl and her mean-looking boyfriend and then be torn to bits? Or did he let go and drop like a stone at the feet of Agnes the sheep and be mashed to a bloody pulp?

She really was out of condition, Mrs. Carmen Sylvester thought to herself as she clambered hand over hand up the last stretch and into the sylvan glade. She must do something about it.

It was with some relief that Shane saw her. At least this rather elderly thirdcomer had a kindly face. "Help," he cried weakly. "Please, please help me."

"Help you?" boomed Mrs. Carmen Sylvester. " 'Out damn spot!' " She used a line she had once heard in some play, grabbed another long, straight branch and joined Belinda with the poking. "Oh, my! This is such fun," she called out.

Shane threw caution — and himself — to the four winds. It was only a matter of a very short time, he reasoned, before all four below him well and truly cooked his goose. Making one of the few right decisions of his morning he launched himself in a flying-fox leap into what he judged to be a softish and deep pile of pine needles. He rolled over and over and down and down, beyond the head and hooves of Agnes and the prodding poles of the two females. This time luck was on his side. He came to his feet much safer than he had been for the last half hour, used three very bad words and took off down the hill in the direction of the town, of Crispin, of Kevin and, above all and most sweetly, Kevin's butcher knife.

* * *

Action, double-quick action, was called for. "We must save her!" Mrs. Carmen Sylvester announced. "The blessed lamb must be saved."

"We been trying to save her for weeks. She's run out of her nine lives, I reckon," said Joe.

"Don't give up! I feel it in my bones, fate is on our side. My morning horoscope told me to be prepared for a windfall. Or was it a landslide? Something big, anyway," said Mrs. Sylvester.

Belinda sat down. "What do we do? What can we do now? Where can we take her? We've run out of places," she said sadly. She patted Agnes's head. "Poor old girl," she muttered.

"Eh?" said Mrs. Carmen Sylvester.

The poor old girl baaa-ed her approval of the attention she was receiving. After all, this had surely been one of the more interesting of her recent mornings.

"We've got to hide her for a while. It'll have to be your shed, Mrs. Sylvester. At least until we can think of somewhere nicer," said Belinda.

"Eh?" said Mrs. Sylvester. "Oh, well. Any port in a storm I guess. Let's just hope the villains don't make their entrance before I've had a chance to clear it out. I've been busy cleaning all my rugs you know. To work! To work!" she cried. "We'll batten down the hatches, wait for the storm to pass and I'll fix us all a nice cup of herb tea." She led the way down the hill singing snatches of her favorite song about nymphs and shepherds.

* * *

Kevin was not at the butcher's shop. "Doesn't work Saturdays. Not during his rugby season," said George, the butcher. "Probably still at home snoring away in bed."

"Will he have his butcher's knife at home with him?" asked Shane, looking in wide-eyed admiration at George's own knife collection jangling at the butcher's waist. Should he, perhaps, borrow one of these for Kevin?

"Eh?" said George.

"I'm sorry, boys," said Kevin's mum, Myra, to Shane and Crispin. "He's around at his friend Bruce's. He's helping polish Bruce's grandma's car and dig a new garden. Will do anything for anyone, that boy. My boy, my Kevin. Would you like a peanut brownie, boys? They're straight from the oven and they're Kevin's favorites."

They found Kevin and Bruce on the doorstep of Bruce's detached flat, sitting in the sun sharing a bottle of beer and looking most unhappy. With five of their rugby team down with the flu and six still suffering from the effects of bones broken earlier in the season, their afternoon sport had been cancelled.

"Piz yoff, mate," Kevin had said. "Whadda we do now?"

"Bumma," Bruce had replied. "Top yup?"

The news carried by Shane and Crispin brought them fully back to energetic life and an absolute frenzy of organizing activity. In twenty-five seconds flat they had Bruce's pickup backed out and around to the front door with Spot, Woofer, Shane and Crispin up on the back under the canopy, and Bruce, Bruce's .22 rifle, Kevin and Kevin's knife in the front. Unfortunately there was no gas in the petrol tank and it took ten minutes of siphoning from Bruce's grandma's very dirty car before they were ready for blast-off.

It was somewhat unfortunate that they had to keep stopping every couple of minutes for Kevin to get out, go round to the back of the pickup, poke his head into the canopy and receive a further set of directions from Shane and Crispin. But no matter. They all enjoyed the solid burn-up round the streets of the town.

"Geez, he sure is a powerful driver, that Bruce," said Crispin as they narrowly missed Father McIntosh in his Honda Civic as he was driving out of the church grounds.

"Hoons! Hoons! That's what they call them. Hoons!" Father McIntosh tooted the horn of the Honda, leaned out of the window and raised a fist in blessing.

"We're gonna get her. We're gonna get her. We're gonna get her," Shane repeated over and over. There was a joyous tone to his voice and a joyous glow on his face.

"Geez! Geez! Listen to those gears, eh? That's a real racing change all right," said Crispin as they took a corner on the wrong side of the road and drew to a very sudden halt. Spot and Woofer fell all over Shane.

They called in at Kevin's home and Kevin had a brief chat with his mum, Myra, who was weeding a few cracks in the concrete driveway. "No, Mum. I don't need me woolly hat, honest. Gonna go t'the dump for Bruce's mum, eh?" and then he poked his head through to Shane, Crispin and the dogs. "Y'okay?"

There were two or three more stops and pokes of his head in through the flap on the canopy. "Zit up air?" was his last one. Yes, it was up there, and in a flurry and spray of stones and mud they dragged to a screaming halt outside the home of Mrs. Carmen Sylvester, Yew Tree Cottage. In no time flat — about nine minutes actually — they had all bundled out, assembled, given each other orders and were making their way up into the pine plantation, hearts pounding exultantly.

"Forgot me ammo," said Bruce to Kevin, patting the pocket of his checked hunting jacket.

"Got me knife, though," said Kevin, patting his hip.

Spot and Woofer were in a seventh heaven of delirious joy. They sniffed out the scents of long-gone rabbits, hares, goats and anything else once living that had run these hills. No matter how loudly, firmly or rudely they were called to heel by their masters, they did precisely as they wished. It was going to be three days before Spot, exhausted, made it all the way back to Kevin's house. It would be even longer before an even tireder Woofer ended up with Mrs. Carmen Sylvester down at Yew Tree Cottage where he was to take up permanent residence. Mind you, these were short periods compared to the seven months Crispin's brother's air rifle would stay hidden from human sight, and even then it didn't make it back to the right hands.

"It's gone," yelled Shane. "They've taken her, eh?" he cried. "They stole her and it's gone, gone, gone," and he burst into a flood of bitter, bitter tears.

"Here, kid. You can use me hanky," said Kevin, kindly.

"Bet I know," said Crispin. "The mad old bat and her carpets."

"Eh?" said Kevin. "Hey, Spot! Spot! Here, Spot!"

"Yeah. Yeah," said Shane, "it's her. She was here and she poked me, too."

"Eh?" said Kevin. "Spot! Here, Spot! C'mon, Spot! Spot! Spot! Spot!"

"Bet she got our sheep. C'mon, Kev. I know where she is. She's down by your pickup. That old house down there. I know. She got our sheep, I know. Gotcha knife, Kevin? Gotcha knife?"

They all crashed down through the trees — all except Spot and Woofer, that is. They went on crashing through the trees up the other side of the hill. It was the scent of blood that made Kevin, Bruce, Shane and Crispin forget all about Spot and Woofer for some long time.

"Yep! Hoof marks! Right 'ere!" Kevin tracked

and they all searched for sign. "There's sign!" yelled Kevin, pointing. Indeed there was plenty of sign because Mrs. Carmen Sylvester had fed almost a whole bed of winter cabbage to Agnes — both lightly cooked and raw. Shane was right. The sign led to the gate of Yew Tree Cottage. It didn't lead just to the gate, either. It led right on inside.

"They got her in there. In there! In there!" Shane's excitement reached boiling point.

"Yeah, Kevin," said Crispin. "Get out ya knife. It's in there, all right."

"Ooooohhh . . ." Shane let out one long, ecstatic sigh. So near. So very near . . .

12
Where Agnes Leads, Others Follow

Belinda and Joe quite enjoyed the herbal tea and natural bran biscuits served up by Mrs. Carmen Sylvester. With Agnes safely shut away in the shed they felt they deserved and could afford a brief rest before planning their next moves. The clatter and noise of Kevin, Bruce, Shane and Crispin, their weapons and their dogs, was long gone up into the pine plantation and Joe had already let the air out of one rear tire on Bruce's pickup. He was mentally debating whether or not to play it safe and do the other three tires when the knock came on the front door.

"Please can I have my sheep? I paid for it," said Kevin, and then, "Please, Mrs. Sylvester," because, firstly he was polite and secondly, he recognized Carmen. Kevin's mum, Myra, had often sewn costumes for Drama Society productions.

"Thou shalt not harm a hair on that holy animal's head." For a moment Mrs. Sylvester did not recognize Kevin. She flung her arms out barring the way and also hiding the view of the outside from Joe and Belinda who stood behind her.

"You don't have to, Kev! You don't have to!" yelled Shane. "You don't have to harm no hair on its head. You can just go straight for its throat, eh?"

"I've come for my sheep," said Kevin again, very politely.

"His sheep," Bruce helped out, swapping his rifle from one shoulder to the other.

"You'd shoot an old, defenseless woman, would you? Well, go ahead, shoot!" ordered Mrs. Sylvester. "See if I care!"

"Shoot her, Bruce! Shoot her! She said you could, Bruce. She did," said Shane, who had forgotten the absence of ammo for the rifle. "Then we'll get the sheep after you shot her."

"It's just me sheep I come for," said Kevin. "Please, Mrs. Sylvester," he pleaded. "I don't want to be no trouble." His mum's lifetime of manners-training was never far from the surface.

Something in the tone of Kevin's voice must have rung a bell or two in Mrs. Sylvester's mind. "Oh, it's Kevin. It's Kevin," she said, lowering her arms. "And how's your poor mum these days?"

This was more than enough for Belinda, who sensed Agnes's life ebbing away almost as quickly as Mrs. Carmen Sylvester and Kevin forged a firm friendship.

"Ya little poo!" she yelled, and ducked round

Mrs. Sylvester and Kevin and out onto the porch to confront Shane Pike. "So! You're outa ya tree eh, murderer? Ya killer!" she added for good measure and picked up a handy garden leaf rake with which she started belting Shane, very, very hard.

Not wishing to be left out of the action or to be seen standing on the sidelines, Joe got busy on Crispin. It took all of Kevin's, Bruce's, and Mrs. Carmen Sylvester's combined strengths to smooth the conflict slightly. As luck would have it, Shane still had Kevin's hanky and didn't have to borrow another. Kevin got down to business again. "Please can I have me sheep, Mrs. Sylvester?"

"His sheep," said Bruce.

"What sheep?" inquired Mrs. Sylvester.

"It's for me mum," said Kevin.

"How nice. A pet for your old mum?" asked Mrs. Sylvester. "How very, very nice."

"Well, sort of something like a pet," said Kevin, who tried not to tell lies.

"His mum'll like it a lot," said Bruce.

"How very nice and kind, and so typical of what I hear of you around town, Kevin," said Mrs. Sylvester.

"It's our sheep. It's his and mine and you're not getting it," said Belinda. "You keep your dirty hands off of our sheep."

"Yeah, bug off!" said Joe. "Don't you listen, Mrs. Sylvester. He's not getting his mum a pet. He's gonna murder her! Murder her!"

"His poor mother?" asked Mrs. Sylvester.

"Surely not. I think there's a law against it."

"He's gonna kill old Agnes. He is, Mrs. Sylvester," said Joe.

"Boys, boys, boys!" said Mrs. Sylvester. "And girl. How on earth did I ever get caught up in this web?"

"I bought it," said Kevin. "I bought it for me dog and me mum."

"It's our sheep," said Belinda. "Old Mrs. Carpenter gave it to us and charged us to look after it."

"What sheep are we talking about?" asked Mrs. Sylvester.

"Please, Mrs. Sylvester, I only want me sheep," said Kevin.

"His sheep," echoed Bruce, feeling a bit left out of the conversation.

"Bet they got it inside," said Shane, and he and Crispin tried to gain entry to the house by ducking around and under Mrs. Sylvester. They were not quick enough.

"Getouta there!" Bash, bash, bash with the leaf rake.

"The old lady entrusted that lamb to their tender care. She is their holy grail," said Mrs. Sylvester. "I think," she added.

"I paid for it, Mrs. Sylvester. I did," said Kevin. "With me own money and all."

"Yeah. Was his money," said Bruce.

"Kev paid for it," said Crispin. "If he wants to

kill it he can. There's no law . . . oooww!" The leaf rake stopped his legal lecture.

"She's evil! Evil, evil, evil. Bad evil . . ."

"Don't you call Mrs. Sylvester evil, you — you — you slug!" Belinda had another bash at Shane.

Shane managed to avoid the worst of her attack. "Savage and vicious and evil! All over! She'd eat a dog, would that sheep."

"Hey, Spot! Spot! Spot!" called Kevin, half remembering something.

"Teeth like razors and she's diseased all over," said Shane.

"She is not diseased. And she's got no teeth, so!" argued Joe.

"She is so diseased! She's filthy diseased," said Shane.

"You calling me mate a liar, are ya?" yelled Belinda, getting more exercise with the leaf rake.

"*Shuddup!*" ordered Mrs. Sylvester. Absolute silence — and this was quite a pity.

"Baaaaa!" said Mrs. Carmen Sylvester's shed, quite loudly.

"That's her! That's her! *That's her! That's her! We found her!*"

Shane led the way. "Getcha knife, Kev! Getcha knife! Go on Kev! Kill 'er! Kill 'er!"

"Baaaaa! Baaaaa!" as the door of the shed was forced open, and careless, forgetful and overstimulated Shane was sent sprawling under the gingko tree, while Crispin came into bodily contact with Agnes for the first time. Bruce stood open-mouthed at the sight of Agnes and hugged his rifle closer to his chest. Kevin made a wild lunge at what was, after all, his property — and well paid for too. Belinda finally managed to break the leaf rake by giving one gigantic "Thwack!" on Kevin's bottom and only a slightly lesser one to Agnes, yelling as she whacked, "Get going, Agnes! It's every sheep for himself!" and then she joined Joe for a quick sit on Kevin until he shrugged them off.

By this time Agnes had done one circuit of the house and garden, had taken a last look at the cluster of her friends and enemies and had made off at a brisk canter, rattling down the road and back to town as Mrs. Carmen Sylvester said loudly, "What the hell have I done to deserve any of this?" and, "Hasn't she realized yet that I'm a vegetarian?" and, "It's taken me seven years to grow that superb scarlet fuchsia!"

Kevin swore crudely and yelled, "GEDDER!"

Bruce swore and raced for the pickup.

Shane cried a little more, swore, and jumped into the back of the pickup.

Crispin swore because everyone else was swearing, followed by Shane and yelled, "Gotcha knife, Kev?"

Joe swore, wishing he had got to the pickup's other three tires when he had first thought of it and took off down the road after Agnes and Belinda.

Mrs. Carmen Sylvester dragged her bicycle out from under a heap of old carpets at the back of the shed, slipped in a patch of recent Agnes droppings, swore, got up, jumped on her cycle and steamed off in the direction of town after Agnes, Belinda and Joe, smelling a little of fresh garden fertilizer.

Wild Sheep Runs Amok in Supermarket was the headline above Agnes's second and last newspaper mention. Once again the human interest level of the sheep world was not considered high enough to warrant a really big headline. However, for those who were there, Agnes's swan song provided a high level of general interest and, for some, just a little pain.

Indeed, most of those who had been touched, one way or another, by Agnes the sheep over the period since the late Mrs. Carpenter's death were present quite by coincidence in the Food Giant Supermarket late that Saturday morning.

Belinda, Joe and Mrs. Carmen Sylvester arrived only moments before Kevin, Bruce, Shane and Crispin, who had been held up (but not for long) changing a wheel on the pickup. Kevin and Bruce had often practiced changing spare wheels in preparation for the motor rallying they hoped to participate in one day.

Agnes the sheep had obviously arrived at the Food Giant before any of the other members of the cast.

Mrs. Walsh and Mrs. Wiggins, Joe's and Belinda's mothers, stood at opposite ends of the bread stands waiting patiently to make a quick grab once Garry, the Food Giant manager, came out to lower, if not halve, the price of that week's leftover bread. They did not speak to each other nor make eye contact, although both of them chatted briefly, albeit separately, to Mrs. Robinson as she hobbled by doing her Saturday shopping.

"It's just amazing how you've settled our Joe down this term, Mrs. Robinson, for all you've got leg problems," said Mrs. Walsh.

Mrs. Robinson, who had not observed one scrap of improvement in the behavior, attitude or work habits of Joe Walsh, was nonetheless perfectly happy to grasp at a word of praise if it was being handed out.

There were no words of praise from Mrs. Wiggins. "I do hope you didn't mind me writing to get our Belinda moved to another class, Mrs. Robinson," she said. "So nice to see your ankle and everything, and it's no reflection on you."

Garry was late reducing the price of bread. His business interview with Derek Pike was taking longer then expected. "I just don't need that land. Not now, Derek. Not with business the way it is. Revenues are down thirty, forty percent since Big Bikkie Bulk Barn opened up down the other end.

Daylight robbery, it is. Not unless you can chop your price on that land, Derek, and then give us a mortgage on top. Business these days . . ." Garry shook his head.

Derek looked out of the window of Garry's office and took little comfort at the sight of Moira, his wife, piling luxury item after luxury item into her supermarket cart. He shuddered.

Kevin's mum, Myra, was in deep and serious conversation with Father McIntosh. The old man seemed unable to move away from her, sandwiched the way he was between the soups and the canned tomatoes. All he had come in for was a bottle of tonic to go with the bottle of gin he had just purchased at the package store next door.

"I blame the homes and the upbringings, Reverend. Really I do. The homes and the motor vehicles and violence and knives and guns. Them and the pornographics. Communities just aren't safe anymore and all of us in our beds trembling, waiting for it. As I was saying to my boy Kevin — you know him, of course — and no mother could hope for better . . ."

"A credit to you, good lady, and now . . ."

"Yes, I am feeling so much better thank you, Reverend," said Myra. "Knitting helps. We've got to put a brave face on it and no one knows like I do." Kevin's mum managed a weak little grin.

The weak little grin was almost electrically, magically, wiped from her face by the sight she saw over Father McIntosh's left shoulder. There, framed for all to see, full-square in the supermarket doorway, was the light of her grim life, Kevin, lovely head of blond hair and all. The blond hair seemed to be standing on end and a blood-red gleam seemed to be slashing like a thousand rays of sunlight across his handsome face as he brandished a knife and yelled at the top of his voice, "Get the . . ." There was a third word but it was mercifully lost in the crash and clatter of ten supermarket carts falling, as Mrs. Carmen Sylvester parked her bike by ramming into them.

Five cars, four cycles, a motorbike and an Allied Farmers' delivery van had ended up on grass medians and in people's gardens in the course of Agnes's middle-of-the-road trot, canter, run and gallop back towards the late Mrs. Carpenter's house and garden. Belinda and Joe had just managed to keep up with the sheep. Mrs. Carmen Sylvester had fallen a little behind when she stopped to help out as best she could with one or two of the minor casualties. Handicapped as they were, Kevin and his crowd did not catch up with Agnes or even spot the sheep until near the supermarket. This was because of Bruce's absolute inability to follow any of Kevin's directions.

Agnes had taken one look at Derek's devastation of her former home, said "Baaaaa" in a tone of disgust and moved on briskly, just at the very moment Joe had bent to tie a length of rope around her neck.

"You've let her go again," yelled Belinda. "Here. Give it to me, useless!"

"Too late," said Joe. "She's gone. Oh, God! She's heading for the supermarket. Oh, God! Please, God, no!"

The gang of four on and in the pickup spotted Agnes as Bruce, following Kevin's directions, was taking the supermarket parking lot at a fairly fast pace as a shortcut back onto the main road. Somehow Bruce had lost the main road two turnings back.

"Sheep! Sheep! Sheep!" Kevin just pointed and panted and grabbed for his knife, while Shane in the back spewed over the tailgate for the third time. Shane was not a good traveller. Bruce parked the pickup against the front pillar and main support of the Food Giant Supermarket.

Against the background of the soft and sweet sounds of imitation classical supermarket piano music the play reached a climax.

Agnes did a quick preliminary circuit of the five aisles of the supermarket. No one stopped her. Had her eyes not alighted upon anyone other than her close friends, Belinda, Joe, Mrs. Sylvester, and maybe even Kevin, everything would have been all right. Regrettably, however, the sight of Shane, Crispin, Derek, and to a lesser extent Mrs. Robinson and Father McIntosh, acted like a red rag to the sheep. Just as Shane yelled out, "Getcha knife out, Kev! We got the old cow," Agnes got to work.

"Thou shalt not touch a hair on her old head!" yelled Mrs. Carmen Sylvester, jumping out from behind detergents and washing powders, and startling Father McIntosh.

"I wouldn't dream of it, dear lady," said Father McIntosh.

"Gedder! She's down here," yelled Shane, racing down the Cakes and Cookies aisle. Agnes found Shane rather than Shane finding her. Almost casually she bent her head. Timing movement to perfection she lifted him neatly and deposited him in Frozen Peas and then piled Crispin in on top of him.

Mrs. Robinson said, "Uurrrghhh . . ." and because of her ankle climbed slowly up a piled mountain of ten-kilogram bags of potatoes that were going out on special.

"Baaa," said Agnes, looking longingly up at Mrs. Robinson.

Agnes did not so much attack Moira, as attack her shopping cart. Weeks later the odd luxury item such as Scottish marmalade was being excavated from under the frozen chickens.

Agnes scored a perfect hit on Derek who on recognizing her had grabbed, of all things, an ax from the hardware display. The ax flew high, described an arc and landed in a beautiful mound of Cook Island tomatoes which were certainly not on special. Derek himself took the full force of Agnes's greeting in the lower abdomen and near the Number Two checkout counter.

"You've squashed all my bread. Now you can damn well pay for it!" said Mrs. Walsh angrily, as Derek slithered across the checkout counter. Garry's new bar code recorder failed to register any bar code stripes on Derek's belly.

Mrs. Robinson was joined by Father McIntosh. As he sat down beside her on top of the potato mountain he unscrewed the cap on his bottle of gin. Mrs. Robinson removed the bottle from his hand before he had a chance to take a swig.

"He's such a good boy. He is!" Kevin's mum, Myra, popped up in Canned Fruit. "Had him potty-trained by two," she called out in Paper Towels and Toilet Paper. "A real man about the house. My boy, Kevin!" in Toilet Soap and Toothpaste. "How are you, Mrs. Sylvester? Just you give me a tinkle when you want some more sewing done."

Garry bleated like a sheep and his staff took a well-earned break from serving customers. Garry paid them so little that most of them were quite happy to lean back and enjoy the action.

Belinda, who had found another leaf rake in Garden Tools, worked hard at keeping Shane and Crispin well frozen.

"You put that clothesline back, Joey. I know you haven't paid for it," cried Mrs. Walsh.

Cans of soup, cans of fruit, of jam, of fish — of everything — tumbled and rolled and added an enormous level of interest and peril to the chase, which ended quite appropriately at the far end of the Food Giant complex and right beside the displays of meats.

Agnes had run out of time, space and breath.

Kevin and Bruce in true-blue rugby-cum-hunting crouches, knives at the ready and making sheep-soothing sounds like, "Here, boy! Here, boy! There's a good boy. Just hold it there nice and still now, boy," between gritted teeth, backed Agnes into a corner from which there was only one way out — past them. They had backed Mrs. Carmen Sylvester into the same corner and they still had to get to Agnes past her. Arms outstretched in front of the animal, Mrs. Sylvester cried, "Thou shalt not touch a hair on her old gray head, nor mine either!" Kevin and Bruce also had to get past Joe who had swapped his clothesline for hedge clippers. Belinda was in there too. Armed with her third leaf rake of the day she had left Shane and Crispin stuck to many packets of peas in the freezer.

Who would have won?

No one ever knew.

Protected by her friends, undefeated in any sense whatsoever by her enemies, Agnes grew tired of it all. "Baaaaaaaa . . ." she bleated for the last time, quietly sat down, rolled over and died.

"She's dead! She's dead! She's dead!" said Joe and Belinda together, crouching and crying over their animal. "You've killed her!" to Kevin. "Now are you happy?"

"Geez," said Kevin, apologetically. "Didn't mean to hurt her, eh?"

"Is there a doctor in the house?" Mrs. Sylvester called, bending down to see if the kiss of life would be of any use. The other actors in the drama gathered around and spoke in hushed voices.

"Well, we done our best," said Joe.

"Yeah. She was old," said Belinda.

From out in the carpark of the Food Giant Supermarket the gruff voice of an arriving customer, or maybe it wasn't a customer, travelled to their ears. "Heel, boy! Heel, I say!" Belinda and Joe looked at each other.

Garry the supermarket manager started to boss everyone around. He also started to look for the owners of the late Agnes. Clearly it was the right time to move before ownership and liability got too carefully worked out.

Kevin and Bruce, helped by Belinda, Joe and Mrs. Carmen Sylvester, carefully — and with not a little difficulty — lifted the late Agnes onto one of the extra large supermarket carts usually reserved for restocking shelves. From there she was removed to the back of Bruce's pickup. Shane and Crispin did not need a lift home.

"We'll get rid of her for youse kids," said Kevin to Joe and Belinda. "Like, I mean, we'll bury her and all that and very nice. Mum's got lotsa flowers. Don't you worry no more. You looked after her good, eh?"

"I do believe you can trust him," said Mrs. Carmen Sylvester to Belinda and Joe. "After all, he's always been so very good to his dear mum." She waved as the pickup slowly disengaged itself from the front pillar of the Food Giant and drove off at a dignified speed.

Afterwards

And then what happened to them all? A quite reasonable question.

Their mission accomplished, Belinda and Joe no longer see as much of each other. After all, it's not as if they were ever close friends and, sadly, it takes more than a sheep to bring people together and keep them there. Doesn't it? Their ownership of the priceless blue-and-white porcelain china does mean they have something in common. Mind you, Mrs. Vi Wiggins, Belinda's mother, is trying hard to do something about that. She's written to the authorities pointing out that the late Mrs. Carpenter obviously made a dreadful, dreadful mistake and that no one in their right mind, not even old Mrs. Carpenter, would place anything valuable in the thieving hands of Joseph Walsh and the whole lot should belong as of natural right to her daughter Belinda. So far the authorities haven't replied so she's written to them again.

These days, Derek, Moira and Shane are economizing. After the falling-through of the sale of his late great-aunt's land to the Food Giant people, Derek is developing some own-your-own flats on the site. He's building them out of old timber (because he's got piles of it) and secondhand bricks from the foundry building at the other end of town that had to be knocked down to make way for the Big Bikkie Bulk Barn. Shane is being used as a laborer by his father on all Saturdays, Sundays and public holidays. It's so much cheaper if you keep things in the family.

Kevin's mum, Myra, came in second in the Mother of the Year contest. She is thrilled to bits with second place prize — a food processor with all the attachments. "After all," she says, "if for any reason our lovely Mother of the Year is unable to fulfill her duties and functions, why, then I shall step into her shoes — and I'm waiting." And much more likely she is to be able to step into the winner's shoes these days. Her fortieth birthday gift, from her much-loved and admired son Kevin, of a hand-cured and beautifully tanned sheepskin floor rug had pride of place right by her bed. Absolute heaven on her arthritic toes and feet. Just so cozy even if the wool on one side does seem a little shorter than on the other.

"People give their kidneys and bits and hearts and junk to be used again by other people before they get buried. Not all the bits of some people get buried. I seen it on the news on the television,"

Kevin had explained to Bruce, some long time ago and just slightly before they disposed of what was left of the late Agnes. Bruce and Kevin have nearly been on their first pig hunt and have been on one Sunday afternoon car rally. It was just as well the next day was a holiday.

Mrs. Carmen Sylvester has put her dog Rambo (once known as Woofer) in a very nice, out-of-town boarding kennel. She is about to leave on an extended overseas tour of the theater capitals of the world, and of Wollongong, Australia, the home of her widowed sister. The cheques from the auction rooms in the city are coming in quite fast and furiously. There seems to be an enormous demand for very old oriental rugs. Once returned from her overseas tour, Mrs. Sylvester has decided she will trade in her bike on a new car. While she's away, the late Mrs. Carpenter's former gardener, Julian, is looking after the grounds of Yew Tree Cottage. "What green fingers that lovely young man has," Carmen has been heard to say. "I'm just amazed at the strange things he can grow."

Mrs. Robinson's ankle has fully mended. She's back to a little light jogging and is thinking of giving up teaching soon.

Everyone else is quite happy and all right. The town gardens are looking a treat, particularly after a damp summer. The damp summer certainly helped in the transplanting of the late Mrs. Carpenter's rhododendrons, camellias and magnolias that many people managed to rescue from her garden in the weeks after her great-nephew Derek took over his inheritance.

"You know that old lady whose sheep me and Belinda Wiggins looked after when she died?" Joe Walsh said to Father McIntosh after helping serve Mass on one fourth Sunday of the month.

"I remember the sheep," said Father McIntosh. "Who could ever forget it?"

"D'you reckon she'll be in heaven, Father?"

"Sheep don't go to heaven, lad."

"I mean Mrs. Carpenter. She wasn't a Catholic, see. She wasn't one of us."

"I remember the old lady well, now you come to mention her." Father McIntosh stroked his chin and smiled. "Quite a dame, that one. Heaven, you say?" Father McIntosh looked down at Joe. "Look, lad, if the late Mrs. Carpenter had her mind set on getting through those pearly gates I very much doubt that the combined forces of Saint Peter and the whole host of blessed saints would have been enough to keep her out." He shook his head again. "Come to think of it, lad, it wouldn't surprise me one little bit if she didn't have that particular blessed sheep with her too!"

About the Author

As a former schoolteacher, William Taylor understands well where projects can lead, although *Agnes the Sheep* is, perhaps, a slight exaggeration. It was in a newspaper article about an enormous butting sheep that he first came across the prototype of Agnes.

Mr. Taylor lives in Raurimu, Mt. Ruapehu, New Zealand. His first book for Scholastic Hardcover was *Paradise Lane*. He has retired from a twenty-five-year career as a principal and teacher and is now writing full time.

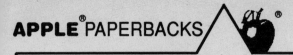

APPLE® PAPERBACKS

Pick an Apple and Polish Off Some Great Reading!

BEST-SELLING APPLE TITLES

❏ MT43944-8	**Afternoon of the Elves** Janet Taylor Lisle	**$2.75**
❏ MT43109-9	**Boys Are Yucko** Anna Grossnickle Hines	**$2.95**
❏ MT43473-X	**The Broccoli Tapes** Jan Slepian	**$2.95**
❏ MT40961-1	**Chocolate Covered Ants** Stephen Manes	**$2.95**
❏ MT45436-6	**Cousins** Virginia Hamilton	**$2.95**
❏ MT44036-5	**George Washington's Socks** Elvira Woodruff	**$2.95**
❏ MT45244-4	**Ghost Cadet** Elaine Marie Alphin	**$2.95**
❏ MT44351-8	**Help! I'm a Prisoner in the Library** Eth Clifford	**$2.95**
❏ MT43618-X	**Me and Katie (The Pest)** Ann M. Martin	**$2.95**
❏ MT43030-0	**Shoebag** Mary James	**$2.95**
❏ MT46075-7	**Sixth Grade Secrets** Louis Sachar	**$2.95**
❏ MT42882-9	**Sixth Grade Sleepover** Eve Bunting	**$2.95**
❏ MT41732-0	**Too Many Murphys** Colleen O'Shaughnessy McKenna	**$2.95**

Available wherever you buy books, or use this order form.

- -

Scholastic Inc., P.O. Box 7502, 2931 East McCarty Street, Jefferson City, MO 65102

Please send me the books I have checked above. I am enclosing $_____ (please add $2.00 to cover shipping and handling). Send check or money order — no cash or C.O.D.s please.

Name_____ **Birthdate**_____

Address _____

City_____ **State/Zip** _____

Please allow four to six weeks for delivery. Offer good in the U.S.A. only. Sorry, mail orders are not available to residents of Canada. Prices subject to change.

APP693